Dear Reader,

Do you have a secret fantasy? Everybody does.
Maybe it's to be rich and famous and beautiful. Or to
start a no-strings affair with a sexy mysterious stranger.
Or to have a sizzling second chance with a former
sweetheart.... You'll find these dreams—and much
more—in Temptation's exciting new yearlong
promotion, Secret Fantasies.

JoAnn Ross continues to delight her many fans with her
sexy and provocative stories. Desiree Dupree unleashes
her secret passions in books...until a series of bizarre
murders leads her to Roman Falconer. He could be
everything she ever dreamed of in a man—unless, of
course, he's a murderer. Experience the appeal and thrill
of the dangerous man.

We find it hard to believe, but 1995 and Secret
Fantasies are almost at an end. We will conclude
this exciting miniseries with Glenda Sanders's
Look Into My Eyes. Please write and let us know
how you enjoyed the "fantasy."

Happy Reading!

The Editors

c/o Harlequin Temptation
225 Duncan Mill Road
Don Mills, Ontario M3B 3K9
Canada

Dear Reader,

New Orleans has always been one of my favorite cities. And although it may be famous for Mardi Gras, if there's a place anywhere in this country that knows how to celebrate Christmas with more flair than The Big Easy, I haven't found it.

Since New Orleans is also a city of contrasts, I decided it was the perfect location to set a Secret Fantasy depicting the dark side of passion. *Private Passions* is the story of a journalist who falls under the spell of a deadly handsome, tormented man who could have been born in the most secret reaches of her imagination. A compelling man who leads Desiree Dupree into a labyrinth of danger and desire.

While researching this story, I experienced a few tense moments myself, when I was caught taking unauthorized photographs inside the police station. Fortunately, everything turned out okay. Except for having to spend the rest of the evening listening to my darling husband, Jay, saying, "I can't believe you did that!" over and over again. But at least he can't accuse me of being boring.

I do hope you enjoy Desiree and Roman's erotic love story.

JoAnn Ross

"Is that really how you see me?" asked Roman. "As a devil?"

Desiree was quite literally trapped, the hard, cold ceramic tile against her back a striking contrast to the disturbingly male body just inches away. A body that radiated warmth and a tightly controlled tension that she found hard to resist.

Desiree stiffened as he reached out. Held her breath as his fingers tightened in her hair. She thought about insisting he take his hands off her, then decided her words would only let him know that his touch was warming her skin beneath her sweater. She'd come here for answers and she refused to surrender what little control she had to this mysterious creature of the night.

"Are you a devil?" she asked.

Roman's eyes held Desiree's with the steely strength of his masculine will. "Sometimes I think I am."

Talented and popular **JoAnn Ross** just keeps delighting her many fans with her wonderful stories. She is the author of over fifty novels, with more than eight million copies in print. JoAnn will be part of Temptation's ROGUES miniseries in 1996, which she will then spin off into THE MEN OF WHISKEY RIVER (also in 1996). Moreover, you won't want to miss JoAnn's next big book from MIRA called *Confessions,* available in bookstores in January 1996.

Books by JoAnn Ross

HARLEQUIN TEMPTATION

482—ANGEL OF DESIRE (Dreamscape)
489—THE RETURN OF CAINE O'HALLORAN (Lost Loves)
506—SCANDALS
537—NEVER A BRIDE (Bachelor Arms)
541—FOR RICHER OR POORER (Bachelor Arms)
545—THREE GROOMS AND A WEDDING (Bachelor Arms)

Don't miss any of our special offers. Write to us at the following address for information on our newest releases.

Harlequin Reader Service
U.S.: 3010 Walden Ave., P.O. Box 1325, Buffalo, NY 14269
Canadian: P.O. Box 609, Fort Erie, Ont. L2A 5X3

JoAnn Ross
PRIVATE PASSIONS

Harlequin Books

TORONTO • NEW YORK • LONDON
AMSTERDAM • PARIS • SYDNEY • HAMBURG
STOCKHOLM • ATHENS • TOKYO • MILAN
MADRID • WARSAW • BUDAPEST • AUCKLAND

To Jan Grammick, in Harlequin's contracts department,
who came up with the offshore bank and
helped Desiree keep her secret.

ISBN 0-373-25662-0

PRIVATE PASSIONS

Copyright © 1995 JoAnn Ross.

1

It was Christmastime in New Orleans. Holiday lights glittered gaily along St. Charles Avenue, twinkled on the towering oaks of City Park, sparkled from the famed wrought-iron railings, flashed on the sides of the historic streetcars and blazed from the *Creole Queen* on the river.

On Bourbon Street, the sounds of Christmas carols, melancholy blues and jazz poured out of open doorways. Along with the usual performers at Jackson Square, musicians had claimed every street corner in the French Quarter, delighting holiday shoppers and revelers with songs of sleigh bells, herald angels and miracles.

In the midst of the festive holiday lights, Roman Falconer's Greek Revival town house was as dark as the inside of a coffin. The house, built French style flush against the sidewalk, was fronted by balconies surrounded by lacy iron scrolling and backed by a shady courtyard. Its damp brick walls had faded to the soft hue of a late summer rose. Roman had bought the house, which was reputed to be haunted, with the royalties earned from his first blockbuster bestseller, *Jazzman's Blues*.

Like a six-year-old anxiously anticipating the arrival of Old Saint Nick on Christmas Eve, Roman had stayed awake until dawn on his first night in his historical-register house, awaiting an appearance from his resident specter.

Five years later, he was still waiting.

A ring encircled a white moon, casting a ghostly glow over the crumbling brick front steps. The shimmering light was more eerie than pleasing.

It also suited Roman's bleak mood.

His head was throbbing. His hands, as he unlocked the moss green front door, were far from steady.

Once inside, he managed to make his way upstairs to his office, where he retrieved a bottle of Irish whiskey and a glass. One of a set he'd received as a Christmas gift last year, the Waterford old-fashioned glass featured an evergreen surrounded by brilliant wedge cuts. He filled the glass all the way to the top of the sand-blasted pine tree.

He'd left his computer on. The phosphorescent light emanating from the screen filled the room with an unearthly green glow. He didn't bother to read the words on the screen. He knew them well.

Too damn well.

He took a long swallow, felt the fire flow down his throat and into his gut and willed his body and his restless, tormented mind to relax. But that was difficult.

Knowing what he knew.

And wondering about the rest.

SOMEWHERE IN the South Pacific, Desiree Dupree was being held hostage by a modern-day pirate who'd boarded her sleek white yacht in the dead of night. Held hostage to reckless passions even more deadly than this dangerously mesmerizing man.

At first she'd fought him, clawing and slashing and screaming at the top of her lungs, despite the fact that there was no one to hear her. In the end, she'd had no choice but to surrender.

She was lying on her back on the smooth teak deck, her bound wrists lashed above her head to the white mast. Her eyes were closed, every nerve ending in her body tingling as her captor's sinfully wicked hands rubbed coconut oil over her naked body.

His voice was low and seductive as he reminded her of all the things he'd already done to her, all the things he intended yet to do—scandalous, outrageous things that both shamed and excited her.

Through half-lidded eyes, she watched his ruggedly cut mouth slowly approach her oiled breasts.

His dark head blocked out the sun. The unwilling anticipation streaming through her made Desiree feel as if he'd touched a sparkler to her heated flesh.

She drew in a breath.

And waited.

The shrill ring of Desiree's bedside phone shattered the still night air, causing her lushly erotic dream to splinter into crystalline pieces.

Cursing, she scooped up the receiver. "Dupree." Her grumpy voice lacked its usual smooth tone. The voice on the other end of the line was equally disinclined to pleasantries. "They've got another rape. At St. Louis Number One. Looks like our boy again."

"How long ago?" Instantly awake, Desiree jumped out of bed, carrying the phone with her as she went to the closet.

"I just picked it up on the scanner. Lucky I had it on, huh?" Adrian Beauvier, her producer at WSLU-TV, added.

"Lucky," Desiree agreed absently as she retrieved a crimson cashmere sweater and a pair of gray wool slacks.

She'd often wondered how LaDonna, Adrian's wife, felt about sleeping with a police scanner sputtering away beside the bed all night. Perhaps that partly explained the departure of two previous Mrs. Beauviers.

Still, Desiree had to admit that Adrian's fanatic dedication to the news had certainly contributed to the station's success. And it had done a lot for her own career, helping her break more than one big story in the five years she'd worked at WSLU. But not one of them had approached the attention-getting potential of this one.

"I'm on my way," she promised.

"I'll have Sugar meet you there."

Sugar, who was known solely by that name, like Cher or Madonna, was a three-hundred-pound African American cameraman whose past exploits included playing offensive lineman for Louisiana State. He'd also had a short career as a professional wrestler, which, rumor had it, was cut short when Sugar couldn't get it through his head that he was supposed to be *pretending* to break his opponent in two.

There was much conjecture around the station as to how he'd come to call himself Sugar, but to Desiree's knowledge, no one had ever gotten up nerve to ask him. He wasn't all that communicative at the best of times; if a conversation seemed to be heading in a personal direction, his renowned glare could cause even the most effusive anchorman to discover a stutter he'd never known he had.

St. Louis Cemetery Number One was bounded by Basin, Conti and Treme streets. Desiree pulled her car in behind the phalanx of police vehicles parked at the curb. The flashing lights atop the cruisers lit the gates of the cemetery in alternating blue and red, reminding her of the revolving color wheel her grandmother had used to illuminate their aluminum Christmas tree back when Desiree was a child.

The tree, like everything else about the Garden District house in which she'd grown up—including her grandmother—had seemed cold and sterile.

A red-and-white ambulance was parked behind the police cars.

Normally at this time of night the cemetery would be deserted, save for those few brave and needy souls who ventured forth to make a request at the tomb reputed to belong to Marie Laveau, New Orleans's voodoo queen of the nineteenth century.

Tonight, however, the uneven sidewalk flanking the cemetery was crowded with sightseers. Desiree flashed her press pass at the uniformed officer and ducked under the yellow crime-scene tape. Her boots made crunching sounds on the crushed shells that served as gravel in this part of the Gulf Coast.

"'Bout time you got here," Sugar said with a grunt. "Typical, though. Poor old Sugar got to do all the work, then the talent shows up just in time for her stand-up."

Desiree's first, knee-jerk reaction was to bristle. Then, remembering that Sugar knew only too well her distaste for the term that suggested she was nothing more than a well-paid pretty face, she managed a shrug.

"Better you turning into a Popsicle than me. Damn, it's cold tonight." She rubbed her gloved hands together.

"You probably not feeling near as cold as that girl in there," he drawled, nodding his shaved head toward the rows of white marble tombs.

The police had set up so many incandescent lamps that the crime scene was lit up like Canal Street during a Mardi Gras parade.

"Start the tape rolling," Desiree instructed Sugar when she spotted a familiar face. "And don't turn it off until I tell you."

"Yes, ma'am, Miz Dupree," he drawled.

Ignoring his sarcasm, she wove her way through the rows of tombs—the above-ground burial necessary due to the city's high water table—to the man running the show. Deputy Chief of Detectives Michael Patrick O'Malley was standing behind a trio of paramedics who were bent over a young woman, obviously the victim. His expression was neither welcoming nor encouraging.

"O'Malley don't look real happy to see us," Sugar observed with his knack for understatement.

"Just keep shooting." As she steeled herself against the icy blue glare, Desiree tried not to think how there'd been a time, not so long ago, when the detective had looked at her in a very different way. "But don't focus on the victim's face."

O'Malley's opening words, like his glower, were definitely less than cordial. "Doesn't Beauvier ever sleep?"

"I don't know. I guess you'd have to ask LaDonna that question," Desiree responded mildly.

"Freakin' guy's like a vampire. Up all night. Speaking of which, why aren't *you* home in bed, Ms. Dupree?"

Despite the circumstances, his voice deepened at the mention of Desiree's bed. He'd been a frequent visitor to that bed for three months, until the combination of his dislike of her producer's penchant for middle-of-the-night calls and constant arguments with Desiree herself had done their romance in.

"I'm a crime reporter, Detective," she reminded him, as she had so many times in the past. Unlike those other times, when she'd admittedly been guilty of screeching at him, her voice remained cool. "Unfortunately, criminals don't always keep bankers' hours."

She glanced past him again, this time catching a better glimpse of a young brunette woman. No, Desiree decided, she was not yet a woman, but a girl poised on the brink of adulthood. She was wrapped in an army green, police-issue blanket; her complexion was white, her brown eyes red-rimmed.

An involuntary shiver ran through Desiree. She felt as if she'd just looked into one of the ghostly white tombs. This had not been the erotic, fantasized forced sex that dreams were made of. This was a harsh, brutal, unromantic rape.

She took a deep breath to clear her head.

"Was she able to give you a description of her assailant?"

"Hasn't said zilch." O'Malley cursed. "The paramedics said she's in shock."

"That's probably not a surprise, considering."

"Probably not," he agreed gruffly. Unlike her, he'd seen the bruises and teeth marks up close. "The kid's lucky to be alive. But she's not a lot of help this way. One of my guys tried to talk to her, but it was like talking to air."

Desiree watched as the medics carried the shock-stricken victim to the waiting ambulance. "Do you know what she was doing in the cemetery at this time of night?"

"She's a working girl. One of the beat cops told me she's been picked up in the last three hooker roundups. She probably brought some john here for privacy."

He glanced around at the crumbling white tombs. "It's not like any of the residents are going to object to the noise."

Though she cringed at his uncaring tone, Desiree knew his gallows humor was merely a cop's way of dealing with the cruel and deadly side of life. "I'll edit that out."

He shrugged. "You'll do whatever the hell you want. You always do."

This was no time to rehash old arguments. "Is it the same perpetrator?"

Another shrug. "Too soon to say."

Desiree saw the familiar wall going up. "But the M.O.'s the same?" she pressed.

"I don't recall mentioning anything about the M.O."

Coaxing more than five words out of Michael Patrick O'Malley at a time was not for the fainthearted. And she'd thought the Irish were supposed to be loquacious.

"What you're saying is that you won't tell me anything."

"You've got more than the rest of the press so far." He glanced back toward the gates and swore. Word had gotten out; other reporters had begun to arrive. "Speak of the devils."

He turned to a uniformed patrolman standing by. "Kolbe, escort Ms. Dupree and her cameraman back to the sidelines. This interview is over."

"Come on, Detective," Desiree coaxed, "give me just one decent quote and I'll go peacefully."

"*How* you go isn't really my concern. Just *that* you go."

And then it appeared, that fleeting expression that let her know she wasn't the only one who sometimes thought about days past.

"Give me a break, Desiree," he said quietly. "If I let you stay here, I'll have to let those jackals in. And pretty soon any bit of evidence I'm trying to preserve will be trampled."

He had, she admitted, a point. "Can we talk later?"

"Lord, I'd forgotten how stubborn you can be when you've got your teeth into a story."

"I want to make sure I get the facts straight. If a serial rapist is loose in the Quarter, people need to know. If not, surely you wouldn't want the citizens of New Orleans to panic if there's no need."

Knowing when he was licked, he muttered a curse—less savage than his earlier one—and caved in. "If I can get away, I'll meet you at eight at the Coffee Pot for breakfast."

"Terrific. I'll even buy."

"We'll go dutch. Wouldn't want the law-abiding citizens of the Big Easy to think their public servants can be bribed with a double helping of Cajun hash and cottage fries."

"Never happen," she said. "You're one of the good guys."

"Keep that thought," he advised her dryly. "Now get out of here before I have to start throwing my weight around."

Desiree allowed a patrolman to escort her back behind the police barricades. "You may as well get some shots of the crowd," she instructed Sugar. "While we're here. Then we can do my stand-up."

"Local color is always good," he agreed.

Hoping that she'd find someone who'd actually seen something useful, Desiree began jockeying with the other reporters in an attempt to interview the spectators. She was headed toward a heavy woman with a cap of frizzy, pewter-colored hair when a movement on the periphery of the crowd caught her attention.

Roman Falconer.

No, Desiree told herself, *it couldn't possibly be him.* Although she was admittedly not familiar with the personal habits of famous, bestselling novelists, she doubted many of them roamed the rougher parts of town in the middle of the night.

Then again, perhaps he was slumming, researching his latest book. Given that Falconer was a teller of tales of murder and mayhem, a serial rapist running loose in the French Quarter would be right up the man's alley.

He was tall and rangy. Borrowing a phrase from the novel she was currently reading, Desiree decided the author had a "lean and hungry" look.

On closer examination, there was no mistaking that the man watching the crime scene with such intensity was indeed Falconer. The first time those mesmerizing indigo eyes had captured her attention had been five years ago, from a pyramid-shaped display of his books in the window of Beaucoup Books on Magazine Street.

The most recent had been tonight, from the back of his latest bestseller resting on her bedside table. Indeed, now that she thought about it, the pirate in her dream had looked a great deal like the mystery writer.

Their gazes met for a prolonged, suspended moment—her amber eyes inquisitive, his cobalt stare dark and oddly haunted.

His clothing, a black leather jacket and black jeans, was starkly austere, giving him the look of a creature of the night. Her admittedly fanciful mind, stimulated perhaps by the crime that had taken place, instantly brought up thoughts of Jack the Ripper. All it would take to complete the image, Desire decided, was a bit of fog swirling around the author.

"Hey! I know who you are!" A strident voice shattered the oddly intimate mood and a woman grabbed

hold of her elbow. "You're that television reporter, Desiree Dupree."

With effort, and from years of training, Desiree managed—just barely—to keep the irritation from her tone.
"Yes, I am."

"You know, you're a lot prettier than you look on television."

"Thank you." Desiree forced a smile. "I think." She
tugged her arm free and turned back toward where she'd
seen Roman Falconer.

But he had vanished.

As quickly and silently as smoke.

2

RETURNING HOME for the second time that evening, Roman went into his study, poured himself yet another drink, opened the French doors and went out onto the balcony. Drink in hand, he watched more patrol cars race to the cemetery. He knew the additional force wasn't necessary. At this stage in the investigation, all that those extra cops could do was muck up the crime scene.

But the sad truth was that beneath the blue uniforms and shiny badges, cops were human, too, possessing the same morbid interest in violence as civilians. That macabre curiosity responsible for the looky-loos at the cemetery tonight also explained the inevitable slowing of traffic at accident scenes.

During his days as a district attorney, Roman had discovered that people were drawn to pain and suffering and death. The more grisly the better. Once he'd decided to write about murders and mayhem rather than prosecute the perpetrators, that knowledge of the human condition had made him a very wealthy man.

In these days of political correctness, his novels had been criticized for their violence. Just last month, a Southern senator had read excerpts from *Killing Her Softly* into the *Congressional Record,* accusing him of glorifying rape and murder. From the press reports, the senator had practically accused Roman Falconer of single-handedly destroying America.

Roman had always shrugged off such criticism. His stories were fiction. Nothing more.

Never once had he felt the need to defend his work.

Not once had he been tempted to apologize.

Until recently. When the French Quarter rapes had begun.

A blinding pain flashed behind his eyes as he looked out across the flat rooftops toward the bright white glow emanating from the cemetery grounds. Last year, when they'd made a movie of *Jazzman's Blues,* the Hollywood studio had filmed some of the location scenes here in the Quarter.

During the shoot, the production crew had lit the same cemetery in the same way, Roman recalled. But on that occasion, when the cameras stopped rolling, the murder victim had gotten up, wiped the fake blood off her face, lit a cigarette and headed off with the rest of the crew to Bourbon Street's jazz clubs.

Unfortunately, recovery would not be so quick, or so simple, for tonight's victim.

Grimacing, he polished off his drink and went back inside for a refill. As he poured the amber liquor into the gaily carved Christmas glass, he caught a glimpse of his reflection in the undraped window.

His face, which had always been angular, was drawn and gaunt. His jaw was darkened with several days' worth of stubble.

He looked, to put it charitably, like the devil.

Which perhaps he was.

His gaze drifted to the computer screen, to the scene he'd written earlier, depicting a teenager bound and gagged in a New Orleans cemetery. Her terrified eyes were wide in her ghostly white face as the man in black performed unspeakable acts upon her naked young body.

Swearing ripely, Roman downed the refill in long thirsty swallows, turned off the damning glow of the computer, then took the bottle and the glass outside, where he spent the lonely hours before dawn looking out over the Quarter toward the cemetery, mired in dark and dangerous thoughts as he proceeded to get quietly and desperately drunk.

THE COFFEE POT WAS bustling. Desiree wove her way through the crowd to a table by the front window that looked out onto St. Peter Street.

"You look exhausted," she said, greeting the detective.

"Believe it or not, I feel even worse than I look."

He stood up and pulled out a heavy oak chair for her. Such automatic masculine behavior was common in the South, and although she considered herself a modern woman, Desiree couldn't deny that she'd missed such chivalry during her college days back East.

He'd already ordered coffee. Steam rose invitingly from two thick white mugs. "Poor baby." She smiled sympathetically and patted his jaw. "Things didn't go well with the mayor?"

His weary eyes narrowed. "How did you know about that?"

"You know as well as I do that politicians' offices leak like rusty faucets."

He took a long drink of coffee, then stared down into the black depths. Accustomed to his habit of choosing his words carefully, Desiree sat back, patiently sipped her own coffee and waited.

"This has to be off the record," he warned.

It wasn't what she'd wanted. But it was what she'd expected. She'd already decided she could deal with that.

All she needed was for him to point her in the right direction.

"Agreed."

His hands tightened around the mug handle, his white knuckles giving away his stress with the situation. "I'm serious, Desiree." His expression was even more grim that it had been last night. "If it leaks out that I've been talking to you about this, it could cost me my shield."

"I won't whisper a word. Cross my heart." She made the childhood gesture in an attempt to lighten the mood.

Her effort failed. He didn't smile. "This latest victim's name is Mary Bretton. She's a sixteen-year-old runaway from Baton Rouge."

Desiree closed her eyes for a brief moment and said a silent prayer for the young girl who had only done what Desiree herself had wanted to do innumerable times growing up. "That's so sad," she said at last.

"You won't get any argument from me on that one." He took another drink of coffee. "It's the same guy."

"Who raped the three other girls?"

The arrival of the waitress to take their orders forestalled his answer. Although Desiree was not normally much of a breakfast eater, this morning, after having worked most of the night, and eager to keep this conversation going as long as possible, she threw dietary caution to the winds. "I'll have a large glass of orange juice, two eggs creole style and a side of biscuits, please. With honey."

Although he lifted a brow at her unusually large order, O'Malley didn't comment. "Bring me tomato juice, a double order of Cajun hash and *callas*," he told the woman, who'd been a fixture at the bustling café for nearly thirty years. After nodding her approval, the waitress refilled the mugs, then left to turn in their orders.

Desiree blew on her reheated coffee to cool it. "If you know it's the same guy, then she must have been able to give you some information."

"Not yet." He dragged a hand down his face. "She went a little crazy during the exam, when the doctor tried to touch her. They've got her under sedation, but the doc said she's blocked out the entire night."

"Then how do you know it's the same man?"

"The M.O.'s the same. He's got a special little quirk."

"You going to tell me what it is?"

"No." At her frustrated look, he said, "It's not that I don't trust you. But I've got to play this one close to the vest."

She knew him well enough to know not to push. "I suppose you've got people out talking to the prostitutes in the Quarter, to see if any of them have had any weirder-than-usual encounters lately."

"Of course. But you know as well as I do that even if there's a hooker out there who's escaped from this sicko, she'd probably write him off as one of the hazards of the profession."

Their breakfasts arrived. He dug into his *callas*—traditional fried rice cakes served with grits and syrup—with all the enthusiasm of a condemned man eating his last meal.

They ate in silence, each lost in thoughts that Desiree suspected were running along the same path. One of the reasons she and the detective had been drawn to each other in the first place was because of the uncanny way they had of often thinking alike.

Except when it came to their individual careers. Michael Patrick O'Malley had not escaped unscathed from his dangerous occupation. Indeed, he'd been shot through the shoulder one night by a kid who was holding up the A&P grocery store on St. Peter's Street as the detective dropped in to buy a pack of cigarettes.

When Desiree had arrived at the emergency room, frantic, he'd shrugged off his injury, saying he'd decided to take the shooting as a sign that cigarettes were indeed hazardous to your health. With the steely strength of will she admired, he'd quit a ten-year habit cold turkey that very night.

However, though he took his own risks in stride, he'd proven unwilling to allow her such freedom, unable to understand why a woman would want to waste her time covering crime stories.

During one particularly memorable—and loud—argument, he'd asked why the hell she couldn't be content to cover feature stories like the birth of a new lion cub at the zoo.

To which she'd furiously countered that perhaps he'd like to turn in his detective's shield and take a job as a meter maid, handing out tickets to people double parking outside the gates of Jackson Square.

Later, they'd apologized. But the rift between them continued to grow, until one morning Desiree had discovered she and Michael O'Malley were standing on opposite sides of a crevasse as wide and deep as the Grand Canyon.

"What time are you going to call the press conference?" she finally asked, breaking the long silence.

"I'm not. Not yet, anyway."

"What?"

"I said I'm not calling a press conference."

She pushed her plate aside, braced her elbows on the crowded wooden table and rested her chin on her linked fingers. "Let me make sure I understand," she said, giving him the probing look that had caused more than one dirty governmental official to belatedly realize that crime-reporter Desiree Dupree was a great deal more than just a pretty face. "There is a serial rapist roaming the French Quarter, attacking young women, and the police department doesn't see fit to warn the citizens?"

He gave her a long, opaque look. "It's not that easy."

"The hell it isn't!" Her emotions, always close to the surface, broke free in a burst of hot temper. Realizing that she'd attracted the attention of a family of tourists seated at the next table, she lowered her voice and leaned toward him.

Desiree couldn't believe he could write off anyone's safety this easily. "I realize the victims so far aren't the most respected members of our society, Detective, but none of those girls deserved to be attacked that way. And the others deserve to know they're in even more jeopardy than usual."

"On that we agree." The only sign of his own aggravation was the tightening of the muscles on either side of his mouth, drawing his lips into a thin, harsh line.

"So, why...?" Her voice trailed off as comprehension sunk in. "This is political, isn't it?"

He gave her a hard look. "This is still off the record."

"Of course." She waved away his warning.

"You already know I just left a long meeting with the mayor.

"Well, the deputy mayor and the commissioner were also there. All three reminded me that the city is entering into our busiest tourist season."

Desiree Dupree was no longer the naive young idealist who had graduated cum laude from Harvard with double majors in journalism and criminal science. Her years working in television had taught her not to expect morality in government. But she couldn't swallow this.

"To put innocent lives in danger just to avoid risking Christmas sales and Mardi Gras revenues is criminal."

"Not the last time I checked the statutes."

"It *is* contemptible."

"Once again, we're in complete agreement."

For a fleeting second his professional mask slipped and she caught a glimpse of the honorable man she knew him to be. "What are you going to do?"

"It's not exactly my call," he reminded her. "The commissioner was quick to point out that we always increase our police force during Mardi Gras anyway. That being the case, there isn't any reason to frighten people unnecessarily."

"Are you going to at least warn the girls on the street?"

"I've been told to keep a low profile," he answered.

"That wasn't exactly my question."

His lips quirked in a ghost of a smile. "Short of sending up flares, or having you announce it on the six o'clock news, I intend to do all I can—given the risks of their chosen profession—to ensure their safety. Which includes catching Mary Bretton's rapist."

It was more what he *wasn't* saying than what he *was* that gave Desiree her answer. Once again he was proving to be absolutely fearless. She knew that the political risk he took by bucking the order to keep the word off the street was nearly as dangerous as any bullet he might have to face. She also understood that to him, solving crimes was intensely personal.

She tossed some bills down on the table and stood up. "Once again you've reaffirmed my faith in mankind, O'Malley."

This time the smile warmed. "Our motto is To Protect and Serve and instill faith in gorgeous TV reporters."

She kissed his cheek. "If it weren't for the subject under discussion, I would have enjoyed this. We'll have to do it again some day. For fun. And for old time's sake."

A shadow crossed his rugged face, chasing away the smile. "I don't know if that's such a good idea, Des."

He was, of course, right. They'd shared too much to ever be able to remain platonic friends. At least while they were both unattached. Nor could they be anything more.

"I really do hate it when you're right." The sparkle momentarily faded from her eyes. "I've got to run. I have an interview to chase down."

"Anyone I know?"

"An old colleague of yours, actually. On the courtroom side of the law. Roman Falconer."

He looked at her with sharp interest. "I didn't realize you ever stooped to doing celebrity profiles."

She wondered what he'd say if she told him that she intended to ask the former-district-attorney-turned-mystery-writer what he was doing hanging around a crime scene in the middle of the night.

Competitive as always, and unwilling to give away a lead, she merely shrugged. "You never know when a story's going to take an interesting twist."

He leaned back in his chair, tilting it recklessly. "Is there something going on between you and New Orleans's most famous citizen?"

"Actually, I've never met the man. He'd already given up public life when I moved back to town. And lately he seems to have become one of those stereotypical reclusive writers."

She flashed him her most innocent smile. "Perhaps you can give me some insight into Falconer. Something that will help me reveal him to my viewers."

"It'll take more than a few anecdotes from me to do that. To tell you the truth, the guy's layered like an onion. I don't think anyone in the department, or even his own office, ever got close to figuring Falconer out. His nickname around the DA's office was the Dark Prince."

When she suddenly remembered the strange, haunted look she'd witnessed in Roman Falconer's midnight-dark eyes, Desiree decided the name definitely fit.

Never one to miss a thing, the detective's eyes narrowed dangerously.

"Well, thanks for the warning," she said with feigned brightness, wanting to escape before he realized that she was being less than forthright with him. "I'll be in touch."

"Of that I've not a single doubt." He tossed some bills onto the table next to hers. "Remember, everything I told you is off the record."

"Of course."

They left the restaurant together, O'Malley stopping at his dented, unmarked police sedan parked outside, Desiree continuing down the street and around the corner, her mind already engaged in framing the questions she intended to ask Roman Falconer.

ROMAN'S FINGERS FLASHED across the keyboard, creating words that chased each other across the computer screen.

His mind was in Exchange Alley, a narrow little passageway on Conti between Charters and Royal streets. During the 1800s, the houses at the corner of Conti and Exchange had been home to renowned fencing masters who specialized in training their clients for that fine old New Orleans tradition of dueling.

Not that they always succeeded. Indeed, several of the masters themselves died on the field of honor, while one of the more enterprising ones covered all bets by opening a cemetery and profiting from those who'd ended up choosing death before dishonor.

The man in black had been known by many names over the ages—Vlad the Impaler, Jack the Ripper, Bluebeard, the Boston Strangler. Whatever name foolish mortals chose to give him, he was, and always would be, a predator. Born with an unquenchable blood lust, he stealthily prowled the back alleys of the Vieux Carre like a panther, stalking his unwitting prey.

There was a roaring inside his head, a raging, cacophonous, mind-blinding storm that could only be silenced by one thing. He slipped a hand into his jacket pocket and touched the handle of the knife, garnering enough calm to focus on his quest.

He was looking for that one special person. A special woman he would take to his special place. And then . . .

Sweet anticipation surged through his blood to pool thickly in his groin. Anticipation hotter than hellfire. More seductive than sex.

Soon.

Roman was suddenly and painfully jerked from his deep writer's trance by a flash of awareness. He walked over to the French doors and looked out. When he saw the woman coming up the narrow street, he cursed under his breath and realized, with a certain sense of fatalism, that he'd been expecting her.

He returned to the computer, saved the new scene and turned the machine off.

Then Roman sighed heavily and went downstairs to wait for Desiree Dupree to knock on his door.

3

THE SUDDEN OPENING of the door, just as she raised a hand toward the gothic, gargoyle-style knocker, caught Desiree by surprise. She drew in a quick breath that immediately caught in her throat.

Those midnight blue eyes, which had seemed so bold in her erotic pirate dream and so strangely haunted last night when she'd seen him outside the cemetery gates, were deeply shadowed, revealing a recent lack of sleep.

Once again he was dressed in stark black, giving him the look of a man who spent his life in the shadows. There was not a hint of softness or gentleness in his grimly hewn face. Shaggy black hair curled over his collar.

"Mr. Falconer?" She thrust out her hand in an assertive gesture. "I'm Desiree Dupree, from—"

"I know who you are, Ms. Dupree," he said, brusquely cutting her off. His fingers closed around hers. "I seldom miss a broadcast. You're very good at what you do."

His voice was as sultry as a steamy New Orleans summer. As he held her hand just a heartbeat too long, those deep tones stirred unwilling, reckless emotions.

She retrieved her hand. "Thank you. I suppose this is where I tell you that *you're* very good at what *you* do. You hooked me with *Jazzman's Blues,* and each book gets more riveting."

At her words, a shadow moved across his face like a cloud across the moon. "That's kind of you to say."

Silence descended.

"Well, now that we've exchanged the obligatory professional compliments, I suppose I should tell you why I've come."

She was smaller than she appeared on television, Roman realized, looking down at her. And far more delicate. Her hair, a dazzling, sunlit copper on the screen, was darker in real life, more of a rich, deep bronze.

"You're not here for a celebrity interview?"

She frowned at his blatant sarcasm. "I don't do puff pieces."

His lips curved in a strangely self-mocking, ironic smile. "Good for you. The news has gotten much too soft in recent years. It's encouraging to meet a reporter who isn't willing to cave in to ratings and popular trends."

When she didn't respond to that backhanded compliment, he rubbed his unshaved jaw. "Well, if you're not here to interview me about my writing, I suppose you want to ask me what I was doing at St. Louis Cemetery last night."

"Actually, I'm talking with many of the people who were there last night." That was the truth. So far as it went.

"But you're especially interested in me. Because I'm the one who seemed most out of place."

She could not deny it. "Yes."

Roman shrugged again. "I've been waiting for you."

He knew that talking with anyone—especially a reporter—about what had happened was dangerous. But there was something about Desiree that had him thinking the risk might be worth it.

Besides, he remembered hearing that she'd been involved with Michael O'Malley, the detective assigned to the French Quarter crimes. If the two of them were still close, it was conceivable that O'Malley, whom Roman recalled having been a driven, never-say-die detective, might share with his former lover some of the details regarding the crimes.

Roman had never enjoyed using people, not even in his days as a prosecutor, when he could at least justify his behavior as protecting innocent people by putting the bad guys behind bars.

But like it or not, it was imperative that he discover what Desiree Dupree—and the police—knew.

Before she could respond, a carriage carrying tourists from Jackson Square pulled up in front of the house. In a jaunty display of holiday spirit, both driver and mule were wearing bright red Santa Claus hats. The tourists—a wife, husband and three kids—stared at Desiree and Roman as the driver delivered his memorized spiel.

"Does this happen often?" Desiree asked in a low voice.

"Several times a day."

She felt strangely vulnerable. It was, she realized, the same way she'd felt during the long-ago custody battle between her aunt and her grandmother, when she'd arrived at the courthouse with the social workers and had been forced to run the gauntlet of reporters. There were times Desiree found it ironic that she'd chosen the same profession as those former tormentors, even though she'd always refused to succumb to pack behavior.

While she was accustomed to talking to thousands of viewers every night on television, and had grown used to fans stopping her on the street and in restaurants, she couldn't imagine tour guides bringing people by her house.

"I suppose a lack of privacy goes with being a bestselling writer."

"I suppose it does," he agreed mildly. "However, in my case, it's the house that's on the tour, not me."

"The house?"

"Like so many other homes in this city, it's supposedly haunted." He waited a heartbeat of a second before adding, "By a slave who was found murdered one Christmas morning."

When he paused again, Desiree had the distinct impression that Roman was purposefully baiting her.

He was.

"She was young and beautiful. She'd been brutally raped, her slender throat slit from one pretty ear to the other."

His eyes held Desiree's with the steely strength of his masculine will. "Later they found six more young women buried in the back garden. All of them had been raped. Then killed in exactly the same way."

Roman watched the horrible recognition shiver through her. "Quite a coincidence, wouldn't you say?" he asked.

If it weren't for the pain in those mocking eyes, Desiree would have thought he was enjoying himself by shocking her this way. "Is it?" she asked. "A coincidence?"

He didn't answer. Instead, his gaze slid back to the carriage, which had yet to move. They could both hear the whir of the father's video camera.

"We'll have more privacy inside," he suggested. He moved aside. "Why don't you come into my parlor?"

Watching him carefully, she lifted her chin in a mute challenge of her own. "Said the spider to the fly?"

The lady had guts, Roman decided. His teeth flashed in another mocking, humorless smile. "Exactly."

The wild idea that Roman Falconer might actually be the man who'd raped pretty young Mary Bretton ricocheted through Desiree's mind.

Telling herself that she was being fanciful again, that the author of all those slasher thrillers was merely having some type of sick fun at her expense, she tossed her head, straightened her spine and walked resolutely through the arched doorway of Roman's haunted house.

Inviting the newswoman into his home had been a spur-of-the-moment decision. One Roman regretted the moment she crossed the threshold.

"Would you like something to drink?" he asked, playing the role of the congenial host as he tried to figure out what to do with her. "Some coffee? Or I think I have some tea bags in the cupboard."

He didn't mention that the tea had been left by a former lover he'd met while researching his current book. A rookie beat cop assigned to the Quarter, Janet Osborne had introduced him to several teenage prostitutes—including each and every one of the rape victims. Roman wondered how long it would be before O'Malley made the connection.

The shutters guarding his eyes had, if possible, deepened. That steady, unblinking gaze made Desiree's mouth go dry. "I'd love a glass of water."

"Coming right up." He gestured toward a nearby doorway. "Make yourself at home. I'll be right back."

Curious about what kind of man would spend his life delving into the dark corners of people's minds, Desiree went into the room, which at one time had undoubtedly been a formal parlor and was now obviously a library.

Mythological figures created in delicate bas-relief decorated the high plaster ceilings. It had been awhile since anyone had cleaned the room. A layer of dust had settled over the antique tables and rolltop desk, and stacks of newspapers were piled up on what appeared to be a very expensive oriental carpet.

Three walls were lined with bookcases, the shelves filled with an eclectic blend of nonfiction and fiction. There was, as she would have expected given his past profession as a prosecutor, an expensive, leather-bound set of law books, as well as numerous texts on forensics and investigative techniques. Telephone books from around the country took up nearly an entire wall, along with several texts on local architecture and customs.

A pair of French doors on the far wall opened out onto a courtyard that was overrun with a virtual jungle of subtropical plants. In the center of the tangled, un-kempt garden stood a crumbling fountain, home to a trio of comely nymphs who appeared to be dancing in the green, algae-choked water.

If Roman was to be believed, this was the same spot where a previous occupant of the house had buried six young women he'd raped, then subsequently murdered. When that thought proved too disturbing to contemplate after last night's vicious crime, Desiree returned her idle attention to the bookcase beside one of the doors.

And that's when she saw it.

Its thin red spine was barely noticeable, hidden as it was between a copy of a latest bestseller and a former president's autobiography.

Private Passions was a small volume of erotic short stories first published in paperback by an alternative press located in San Francisco. When the book garnered unexpectedly high sales, rights were sold to a New York publisher, who reissued the slim text in hardcover. Response to the stories had proved overwhelming.

One tale in particular—"Scarlet Ribbons"—drew a remarkable number of frank letters from female readers relieved to discover they weren't alone in indulging, during their most private moments, in a secret, age-old rape-bondage fantasy.

Indeed, so many women wrote to the publisher demanding more such stories that the anonymous author—known only as Mirielle—had gone on to write a sequel entitled *Fears and Fantasies*. Published this past July, it was already in its fifth printing.

Desiree took the slender book from the shelf, but did not open it. She was more than a little familiar with the sensual stories. She should be, having written them.

Although most of the fan letters the publisher had forwarded had been from women, enough had been written by men to reveal that the appeal of erotica written from a woman's point of view went beyond female readership. Still, finding her book—which was incredibly personal to her—in the private library of a man whose work she was currently reading seemed more than coincidental.

Desiree's first encounter with erotic literature had been when she'd run across a rare collection of Victorian erotica stashed away in a dusty corner of a used bookstore on Decatur. The stories, written over a century ago, had stimulated sensual fantasies she'd never known were lurking in her subconscious.

When she wrote a few of them down for her own amusement, it was as if a dam had burst. Once set free, her imagination created more and more erotic tales—stories she never considered trying to get published. Until the day she covered a demonstration outside the home of a local author known for writing erotic literature.

The parade of placard-carrying protestors, accusing the writer of all sorts of heinous crimes and warning her of hellfire and brimstone, had been topped off with a symbolic book burning that had gotten the leader of the radical religious group arrested and had made for very good television.

No fan of censorship, Desiree had interviewed the writer on the following night's newscast. Later, over coffee after Sugar had packed up his minicam and left, Desiree had admitted to having written a few erotic stories herself. When the author gave her the name of a small publishing house in San Francisco, Desiree assured her the stories had not been written for publication. That was when the slender brunette, who certainly did not look like the pornographer her detractors were calling her, had reminded Desiree of how much pleasure she'd derived from the stories she'd read. Perhaps others would receive the same pleasure from *hers*, she'd suggested.

So Desiree had typed them up and sent them off as a lark, and had been stunned when the acceptance phone call came six weeks later. And now, although she'd never planned for it to happen, she'd become a popular—albeit anonymous—writer of erotic fiction.

Not wanting to be caught with this particular book in her hand, Desiree replaced it on the shelf and sat down in a fancifully carved antique hunt chair across the room.

A moment later Roman returned with a tall tumbler in his hand.

Her scent, which hit him the instant he walked into the library, was every bit as enticing as Roman suspected this woman he invited into his bedroom every weekday night through his television screen to be.

"I seem to have run out of ice cubes."

Her intelligent topaz eyes were thickly lashed and home to gold facets that radiated outward like the rays of the sun. He wondered why he'd never noticed her eyelashes before and decided that the intense glare of the studio lights undoubtedly overwhelmed them. A scattering of freckles, also undetectable on television, were sprinkled across her cheekbones and the bridge of her slender nose. Her complexion was the true, almost-translucent ivory of a natural redhead.

Her mouth was wide and mobile, her painted lips as red as ripe berries. The way they'd parted on a surprised gasp when he'd first opened the door had made him—a man who rarely gave in to impulse—want to taste them to see if they were as sweet and succulent as they appeared.

"I apologize for not being a better-prepared host," he said instead.

"This will be fine." Unnerved by the way his gaze had settled on her mouth, she took a sip.

Although the library was comfortably spacious, the man literally overwhelmed it with his subtly dangerous masculinity. Seeking something—anything—to say, Desiree dragged her gaze from his and glanced up at the intricately carved woodwork.

"This is a marvelous house," she said honestly, deciding to overlook the layer of dust, the copies of the *Times Picayune* piled up on the carpet and the overgrown garden that could easily be cleaned up with a few days' hard work. "I can see why you bought it. Despite the alleged ghost."

"The ghost was not a liability. On the contrary, I found it one of the more appealing selling points. Unfortunately, there hasn't been so much as a blood-curdling scream or a rattling chain since I moved in."

She thought about the story he'd told her, made the inevitable comparison between the victims of one of the previous owners of this house and the girl last night and shivered. "You find rape and murder appealing?"

"Not appealing," he corrected. "But most people have a primal attraction to violence."

Desiree frowned, thinking back on the crowd that had gathered last night. "That's not a very comforting idea."

"Not comforting, perhaps. But true. How else would you explain the success of *Rambo* movies, and all the other so-called male adventure films they spawned?"

"Those movies are geared solely to male adolescent fantasies."

"Granted." He smiled in a way that left her feeling uneasy. Almost set up. "But surely you're not saying that women don't also fantasize about violence?"

"As a rule, I don't think the average woman fantasizes blowing up buildings."

"That's probably just as well," he decided. "But although I'm no expert in the workings of the female mind, I'll bet more than one woman has incorporated a bit of controlled violence into her sexual fantasies."

Currently working on her third book, entitled *Forbidden Fantasies*, Desiree found herself on suddenly shaky ground. Her royalty statements were proof that women's fantasies were a great deal more uncivilized than the men in their lives might suspect.

When she felt her emotional side responding to Roman's deep, dark look, she knew it was time to change the subject. "As fascinating a topic as this is becoming, I'm afraid I'm due at the station for a staff meeting soon," she said, briskly returning the conversation to her reason for having come here in the first place. "Could we please discuss last night?"

"Of course." Behaving like a man who had nothing to hide, Roman sat down across from her, linked his fingers behind his dark head, spread his long legs out in front of him and said, "Ask away."

4

DESIREE TOOK a notebook from her leather shoulder bag and crossed her legs, making Roman wish she'd chosen to wear a skirt instead of those charcoal gray flannel slacks. The brief, unbidden charge of sexual interest provided a welcome respite from the dark thoughts he'd been inflicted with lately.

Noticing a beautiful woman's legs was a perfectly normal male reaction. Perhaps he hadn't gone completely over the edge.

Yet.

Desiree saw the flash of attraction in his eyes and felt a responding twinge. She'd been comfortably celibate for months. This was not the time, she scolded herself firmly, for a flare-up of hormones.

"Why don't we begin by you telling me what you were doing at the cemetery?" she suggested.

"I was taking a walk. When I saw the patrol cars, I decided to wander over and see what all the commotion was about."

"Do you always take walks in the middle of the night?"

"Sometimes, when I'm working on a book and the words stop flowing." His eyes returned to hers and lingered. "Do *you* always smell so damn good?"

Desiree found the slanted half smile that had replaced his usual remote glower distractingly appealing. Reminding herself that she'd come here for answers, she refused to surrender what little control she had of the situation. "I believe I'm the one asking the questions."

"Point taken," Roman said agreeably.

"So you arrived after the police?"

"Asked and answered," he responded in the court-room jargon that reminded her he was more than a little familiar with interrogation techniques. "I already said I was drawn to the cemetery by the police cars."

"So you did. I suppose that also means you didn't see anyone leaving the scene of the crime?"

"If I were a witness to a crime, Ms. Dupree, I would have probably made a fool of myself by trying to appre-hend the perpetrator. At the very least I would have called 911 and stayed with the young woman until the police arrived. You certainly wouldn't have had to track me down."

"Yet when the police did arrive at the scene you didn't stay."

"There was nothing I could do to help. I'm no longer a prosecutor," he reminded her. "There was no reason for the cops to talk with me."

"I find it difficult to believe that not one officer at the scene would have been willing to discuss the crime with you. Given your former position."

"I didn't say no one *would* talk with me. What I said was there was no official reason for me to interrupt an investigation."

"That's very considerate of you," she said dryly.

Although she represented more trouble than he needed, Roman liked the fact that this reporter with the exquisite face was no pushover. "Consideration had nothing to do with it. There were already enough peo-ple who didn't belong there wandering around. I had no intention of compromising a crime scene and blowing the case for Detective O'Malley."

From the way his gaze turned vaguely accusing, Desiree suspected that she and Sugar were two of the interlopers he was referring to. "I had the feeling," she said, trying a new tack, "that you didn't want to be on camera."

"You're right. Because we both know that the situation would have become macabre theater—you interviewing the writer of so-called slasher novels in the middle of the night, outside a cemetery where a young girl had just been attacked. *I* would have immediately become the story, which would have shifted attention away from trying to find the rapist."

That made sense. Still, every instinct Desiree possessed told her that there was more behind his disappearing act than he was saying. "Do you know the victim?"

He shrugged. "I've no idea."

"That's not really much of an answer, Mr. Falconer."

"Call me Roman. And it's the only answer you're going to get." His expression was unnervingly calm. "Unless, of course, you're prepared to tell me her name."

He'd boxed her into a very neat little corner. Michael had contravened policy by telling her the girl's name in the first place, on the condition that the revelation be kept off the record.

"The police haven't released her name yet."

"But you know."

"What I know isn't really up for discussion."

Roman gave her points for trying. But it was obvious that O'Malley had already shared aspects of the crime with her. Over breakfast? he wondered. Or perhaps even earlier, like in bed?

He imagined her soft and warm, her Titian hair tousled from sleep, tumbling over her bare shoulders, her remarkable gilt eyes gleaming with the satisfied glow of a woman who'd experienced some predawn lovemaking.

Telling himself that he had no interest in who this woman was sleeping with, Roman realized that the inside access to the rape investigations he'd been seeking had just providentially come knocking on his door.

And as risky as it was, given his involvement in the crimes, he was going to have to stay close to Desiree Dupree. At least until he discovered what, exactly, Detective Michael Patrick O'Malley knew.

"So, what you're saying is that your being in the vicinity of the crime was only a coincidence?" Desiree asked, pressing on.

She looked so earnest, despite the seriousness of the situation, that Roman couldn't resist a faint smile. "If we were in court, you could be accused of leading a witness, Ms. Dupree."

"Ah, but we're not in court."

"True." He nodded, acknowledging her point. "I live in the Quarter." His shoulders lifted in a careless shrug. "Sometimes I walk at night. It's not the first time I've come upon a crime scene. And, unfortunately, it probably won't be the last.

"And as much as I enjoy being visited by a lovely woman who smells of night-blooming flowers and midnight trysts in the Casbah, I'm afraid that, if you've come here looking for answers, I'm not going to be a lot of help."

Once again instinct told her that he was holding back. He might be a former district attorney, turned bestselling author. He may have powerful political friends, including his father, a state supreme court justice, and his mother, a respected professor of law at Tulane University.

But if Roman Falconer thought Desiree was simply going to throw in the towel because he was making things a little tough for her, he had another think coming.

She put her notepad into her bag and stood up. "I appreciate your having been so candid with me, Mr. Falconer." Her dry tone said otherwise. "And I apologize for taking you away from your writing."

"It was time for a break anyway." He stood up as well. "I just had an idea."

"Oh?"

Roman would have had to be deaf to miss the skepticism in her tone. Despite the risk she represented, he found himself almost enjoying himself. Enjoying her.

"Why don't I spend the afternoon thinking about last night? Trying to recall any small details I may have overlooked? I'll drop by the station after your six o'clock newscast and we can go discuss whatever I come up with over some casino oysters at Brennan's."

The suggestion, along with his sudden change in attitude, set off warnings sirens. Alarms that were both personal and professional. "Are you asking me out to dinner?"

"We both have to eat. So we may as well do it together while discussing what I remember about last night."

"But how do you know if you'll recall anything?"

"Good point." His smile was slow and dangerously seductive. "So why don't I just drop the pretense, tell you I find you immensely attractive and would very much like to spend some time with you?"

Once again Desiree had the feeling he was giving her only a half truth. "I'm sorry, but I've already promised to appear at a charity auction for the station."

He wasn't surprised by her refusal. Neither was he deterred. "You work a rough schedule. Out in the middle of the night, running down a story the next morning, then a charity event."

"I don't have any reason to complain."

"Neither, I suspect, does station management." He put his hand on her back and began steering her toward the front door. "Especially since, after you began filling in for Meredith Courtney, the station crushed the competition in last month's sweeps ratings."

Meredith Courtney was an evening anchor who'd taken a six-week maternity leave upon the birth of her young son. Although Desiree knew that most newscasters would probably sell their grandmothers to win an anchor spot, she found the role confining. And boring.

She thought about insisting that he take his hand off her, then decided a display of such prickly behavior would only let him know that his touch was warming her skin beneath her sweater. Like him, she opted to keep some secrets to herself. "We were lucky," she murmured as he opened the front door.

"Luck had nothing to do with it. And neither did that empty suit they've got you partnered with. It was all you."

She was standing on the front step now, looking up at him while he gazed down at her. Even as she opened her mouth to defend her co-anchor, Desiree found she couldn't. Because she'd used that same unflattering description of John Keating herself, in private conversations with close friends.

"You really do watch the newscast," she said instead.

"I told you, I wouldn't miss it." He was no longer touching her, but his eyes, as they took a slow tour of her uplifted face, possessed all the sensual impact of a caress. "Beauty and brains is a lethal combination in any woman. It's also highly irresistible."

"I'm disappointed," she said in a cool voice designed to hide the fact that his intimate look and black-velvet voice had her heart hammering. Her fingers tightened around the leather strap of her shoulder bag as she reminded herself that her visit here today was strictly business.

When he arched a questioning brow, she said, "I would have thought a writer whose books were on the *New York Times* bestselling list could have come up with a more original pickup line."

Roman laughed at that, enjoying the much-needed release. "Next time."

His laugh was rough and harsh, almost rusty, as if it hadn't been used in a very long time. Desiree could have taken his words as a promise or a threat. Strangely, she thought them to be a bit of both. Once again her emotions bubbled dangerously close to the surface. Once again she tamped them down.

Not trusting her voice, she merely nodded, then turned and walked away.

As he watched her stride toward her car, parked across the street, Roman enjoyed the smooth movement of her slender hips in those tailored slacks and found himself wondering yet again if Desiree Dupree's legs were as appealing as the rest of her.

He stood in the doorway until she'd driven away. Then he went into the house, returning to the library to make a phone call.

"Hi, Mom?" His voice was filled with an easy, genuine affection that Desiree, were she to have been eavesdropping, would have been stunned to hear. "You know that charity shindig you've been trying to talk me into attending?"

Roman listened patiently to the familiar litany of complaints. Despite a demanding career, not to mention the social obligations that came with being the wife of a state supreme court justice, his mother had her manicured fingers into myriad community pies. Roman had long ago decided that, as much as he truly loved this woman who had taken him into her home and raised him as her own, if he caved in at every invitation to her various fund-raising functions, he'd never get any work done.

"Well," he said, when she finally wore down, "if I'm still invited, I've changed my mind."

AFTER A LONG DAY chasing down witnesses, and a six o'clock newscast in which gremlins seemed to have taken over the TelePrompTer, causing it to alternate between racing through the script and dragging it out nearly word by word, all Desiree wanted to do was go home, soak in a bubble-filled tub with a glass of white wine and a trashy novel, then fall into bed. Unfortunately, her day was far from over.

Fortunately, she was a very good actress. No one in the New Orleans Riverfront Hilton's Rain Forest Room, privately booked for this occasion, would have suspected that she was dead on her feet.

The fact that she was here to take part in a celebrity auction was not so unusual, given her station's reputation for supporting local charities.

What *was* different was that instead of the usual assortment of goods and services donated by New Orleans's business establishments, high-profile single men and women had been placed on the auction block.

Amidst a virtual jungle of greenery, Desiree sat at her table, located near the front of the room, and nursed a single glass of champagne all evening, while making small talk with contributors who'd paid $500 for the privilege of bidding on a dream date with one of the participants. All hopes of sneaking away early had been dashed when she'd been handed the tasseled program, and seen that her name was listed last.

Unsurprisingly, the prices escalated as the liquor continued to flow. Two young women nearly came to blows over a hunky, morning-drive-time deejay, while a junior partner in a prestigious law firm, competitive to the end, offered to throw in his Rolex to keep from being outbid by a vice-president of Hibernia National Bank for an attractive blond caterer.

Finally, it was Desiree's turn. Reminding herself that it was for a good cause—who could argue against health clinics for the working poor?—she made her way to the stage, where she was forced to smile as the auctioneer touted her various accomplishments, including a regional Gulf Coast Emmy for last year's five-part series on crime and gambling.

"Ms. Dupree is offering a French Quarter gourmet music fantasy tour night, beginning with cocktails at Napoleon House, on to an exquisite, specially prepared dinner at the grande dame of New Orleans restaurants, Arnauds, followed by some R & B at the House of Blues, ending up with café au lait at the Café du Monde on the levee."

He sighed appreciatively. "All this and Desiree Dupree, as well. Any man would be in heaven." A murmur of agreement swept the room. "Gentlemen, let's begin with five hundred dollars."

Having watched the bidding rise to as high as five thousand, Desiree was not necessarily surprised when the starting price was easily and quickly met. She was, however, more uncomfortable and embarrassed than she'd ever been in her life.

As she stood on the stage surrounded by *faux* jungle scenery, a smile pasted on her face, she found herself wishing that she'd chosen to wear her chic black-and-white satin tuxedo suit, as originally planned.

Instead, at the last minute, her hand had reached into her closet and pulled out the scarlet dress shot with gilt threads. Cut like a slip, it skimmed her body, ending high on the thigh, while leaving her shoulders and back bare, revealing her attributes in a blatant way that made her feel like a headliner at one of the stripper clubs on Bourbon Street. She wondered if anyone could see that her legs were shaking.

As the bids escalated into the stratosphere, she closed her mind, concentrated on getting through this humiliating event and vowed that the next time the station manager signed her up for an appearance without asking her first, she was going to smack him.

"I have fifteen thousand dollars," the auctioneer was saying when Desiree reluctantly tuned in again, "from the gentleman in the third row."

"Fifteen five." This from a man seated two tables away who'd been blatantly staring at her all evening.

"Sixteen," called the man who'd been seated beside Desiree at the table. A former wildcatter who'd made it big in bayou oil, he'd ignored the black-tie instructions on the invitation, showing up in a Western-cut suit studded with silver and turquoise. He'd been drinking Sazeracs since before she arrived, his behavior becoming more and more obnoxious until she'd finally had to tell him—discreetly, of course—that if he put his damp hand on her leg one more time, she'd have no choice but to dump her champagne in his lap.

"I'll bid sixteen five," the oilman's opponent countered.

Her drunken tablemate was obviously unaccustomed to being bested. "Eighteen."

Desiree held her breath, praying for someone—anyone—to top that. But instead the other bidder threw up his hands and surrendered, causing Desiree's heart to plummet.

"I have eighteen thousand dollars," the auctioneer was saying. "And we're going . . ." Desiree felt her smile slipping by notches " . . . going . . ."

"Twenty-five thousand dollars," a deep voice suddenly offered.

The drawl was all too familiar. Desiree whipped her eyes to the back of the room. Usually she found men in black tie sophisticated and sexy—like Cary Grant in *To Catch a Thief*. In Roman Falconer's case, the custom-tailored tuxedo only served as a vivid contrast to his rampant masculinity.

Their eyes met—his dark and sardonic, hers narrowed with annoyance at his grandstanding. The next thing she heard was the sound of the oak gavel striking the podium.

"Sold, to Mr. Roman Falconer, for the sum of twenty-five thousand dollars."

The room exploded with applause and excited conversation.

Conversation that ceased, row by row, as Roman made his way toward the stage.

"Ms. Dupree." His eyes gleamed with masculine purpose and his lips curved in a wicked smile. "I believe this is our dance."

On cue, the band began to play. Realizing that every eye in the room was locked on them, Desiree forced a pleasant smile that belied the veiled censure in her eyes and descended the steps.

As he'd done that morning, Roman placed his hand against her back, the gesture unmistakably possessive as he led her out onto the dance floor. Desiree was relieved when other couples streamed after them.

Her skin was soft and the fine bones of her hand felt incredibly delicate in his. After a few steps, Roman leaned back and let a blatantly masculine glance roam over her. The dress, as scarlet as a defiant flame, hugged her slender curves. He'd been pleased to discover that her legs, clad in a pair of sheer stockings, were every bit as long and firm as he'd fantasized.

"You truly are a stunningly beautiful woman, Desiree." And well worth every penny he'd promised to pay to his mother's beloved charity.

"Thank you." From the time she'd finally escaped puberty at fourteen, emerging from a cocoon of braces, freckles and sharp childish angles into a bright and dazzling butterfly, Desiree had been flattered by countless men. But never had such masculine praise fluttered her nerves as it did now.

"It's the truth." He drew her back to him. Visible through the room's glass wall, a stately white cruise boat, lit up like a Christmas tree in white, red and green, made its way up the Mississippi River. "The whole truth and nothing but the truth."

Desiree flatly refused to be charmed. "I didn't realize you were going to be here tonight."

"It was a last-minute impulse." He brushed his cheek against her cloud of tawny hair and drew in a deep, pleased breath. "Lucky for you, huh?"

She fit in his arms a bit too perfectly for comfort. When she felt herself tempted to lean her head against the firm line of his shoulder, Desiree stiffened. "I'm not sure I get your drift."

"If I hadn't shown up in the nick of time to buy you, you would have ended up spending a fantasy evening with some creep whose idea of foreplay is groping your leg beneath the tablecloth."

Knowing a writer's penchant for observation, Desiree was not all that surprised that he'd noticed—or guessed—the little drama that had taken place at her table. But there were a few points she felt obliged to clear up.

"For the record, you didn't buy *me*. You merely paid for my companionship for one evening."

"And you've no idea how much I'm looking forward to it." Knowing he was being obnoxious, he skimmed his hand up her bare back.

"Are you always so rude?"

"Since when is telling the truth being rude?" He deftly twirled her past the banker and the caterer.

"Suggesting that sex is part of the bargain—"

"Objection, your honor. I don't recall mentioning sex."

"I suppose I imagined that reference to foreplay?"

"Ah." He smiled and drew her closer. There was a lean and dangerous power to his body that Desiree found more deadly than mere brute strength. "I was referring to the painfully obvious plans of that poor-man's J.R.

Ewing who seemed so enamored with you. Believe me, Desiree, my intentions toward you are absolutely honorable."

His smile was enticing, but unwilling to give Roman the upper hand, Desiree again refused to be charmed. "Isn't that what the wolf told Little Red Riding Hood?"

He shook his head in mock regret. "You sure are a tough nut to crack, Desiree Dupree. Fortunately, we're going to have a great deal of time to get to know one another—" his fingers played with the ends of her hair "—on our date."

"About that—"

"You're not thinking of welshing, are you?" He tilted his head to look down at her again. "And deprive all those poor, ill children of much-needed medical care?"

"You're a rich man." The idea that he believed his wealth had purchased her, as her grandmother's fortune had done so many years ago, irked. "Why can't you just send in a check?"

"What makes you think I haven't?" When she glanced up at him, clearly surprised, he gave her another of those unnerving, sardonic smiles. "My mother is a very persuasive woman. I've already made a generous contribution.

"My offer this evening was for a fantasy night with New Orleans's sexiest crime reporter." He released her hand and skimmed a long dark finger down her cheek. "Surely you wouldn't want me telling Barry Collins that his star reporter and much-respected anchorwoman was refusing to keep her word?"

Barry was her station manager. And her boss. She should have known, since both men grew up in New Orleans, that they'd know one another.

"You realize, of course, that what you're suggesting is coercion," she murmured.

Roman wondered if she realized that those cool round tones only made the passion in her eyes seem hotter by comparison. Before he could respond to her accusation, a low, deep rumble of thunder echoed, followed by several startling cracks of lightning that lit up the suddenly darkened room.

As the simulated indoor storm that gave the Rain Forest Room its name proceeded to delight the crowd, Roman lowered his head and kissed her.

5

ROMAN'S MOUTH ROAMED over hers, slowly, softly. Desiree knew that she could have stopped him. Even now she could step away and he would have to let her go. But his lips were so clever. So tempting. The tender, nibbling kisses lulled her into complacence, even as they excited. Murmuring something she couldn't hear over the clap of thunder that literally shook the room, he drew her closer. His surprisingly gentle, yet confident hand stroked her bare back, creating a trail of heat up to the nape of her neck, before retreating again to her waist.

The pleasure was liquid, as warm as a tropical rain. Her senses swimming, Desiree had no choice but to cling to him, enjoying the stolen kiss for the sheer pleasure it brought her.

Having expected a flare of passion, Roman was unprepared for the tenderness flooding through him. Time ceased to have meaning. He could have kissed her endlessly.

Her sultry, mysterious scent of oriental flowers and incense surrounded him, bringing to mind veiled, ebony-eyed harem women lounging about on tasseled pillows. Her taste was as potent as whiskey, as drugging as opium.

And then, just as quickly as it began, the simulated rainstorm ended. There was scattered applause for the dazzling special effects, then the band began to play again and everyone resumed dancing.

Everyone but Roman and Desiree, who were standing in the center of the dance floor, oblivious to the other couples swirling around them.

Desiree was the first to speak. "Why did you do that?"

The answer was too complex to go into in such a public forum. Especially since Roman wasn't certain he understood all the feelings that had unexpectedly been stimulated by the kiss he'd been fantasizing about ever since Desiree Dupree had shown up on his doorstep this morning.

"We've both been wondering what it would be like—"

She knocked away his hand when it began playing with her dangling gold earring. "I haven't." All right, so it was a lie. But she was definitely not prepared to share her secret fantasies with this man.

"I stand corrected." His lips curled in a wicked, knowing smile that assured her he knew she was being less than truthful. "*I've* been wondering what it would be like. So it seemed like a good idea to get it out of the way before our date."

She let out a long breath. "I think, if you're going to insist on going through with this ridiculous date you've overpaid for, it's important to set some ground rules."

Like it or not, they were already beyond setting rules and limitations. But if it made her feel safer . . .

"The first rule is you're not allowed to have any more ideas." She tilted her chin and flashed him a challenging gaze. "I may have to go out with you. It is, after all, for charity. But no amount of money gives you any right to manhandle me."

Manhandle? Roman was sorely tempted to point out exactly whose slender arms had wrapped around his neck.

"Agreed." He nodded and resisted the urge to kiss her senseless, just to prove he could make her forget all about her stupid damn rules. "What else?"

Although his voice was calm, there was a flare of hot, ripe emotion in his eyes that intrigued and unnerved her. All the other regulations she'd been prepared to list left her mind, like words wiped from a glass slate.

"Why don't we go somewhere else and discuss this," he suggested when she hesitated. "Somewhere more private."

"Like your place?"

"Or yours." He shrugged. "Whichever. Though my house *is* closer."

"How do you know where I live?" A chill ran through her, replacing the warmth his kiss had instilled.

Her cheeks, which had been flushed from the shared kiss, turned as pale as sleet. Although the band was playing something slow and dreamy, Roman could feel the mood slipping away.

"It wasn't that difficult. I made a few calls—"

"A few calls?" Realizing her raised voice was drawing unwanted attention to them, Desiree shook her head and walked off the dance floor, leaving him to follow her to a secluded spot beneath a gnarled indoor cypress tree. "A few calls?" she repeated in a low, furious voice. "What the hell gave you the right to do that?"

"I wanted to know about you."

His lack of remorse at invading her privacy was almost as infuriating as his actions. "And do you always get what you want?"

"Not always." The passion in her eyes and on her face intrigued him. Enticed him. "But most of the time, yes." He opted for honesty. "And I'm not going to apologize for wanting you, Desiree."

She dragged her hair back from her forehead. "Lord, you have a lot of nerve."

She welcomed the return of anger that steamrollered over her earlier fear. Having suffered a stalker last year, she found the idea of any viewer—especially a male viewer—knowing where she lived more than a little unsettling. "And I'm afraid this is one time, Mr. Falconer, that you're going to be disappointed."

That said, she turned on her heel and marched toward the bank of elevators. Roman considered going after her, then decided there was no point in pushing her any further.

There would be another time; he'd already ensured that with a hefty check. That was enough. For now.

The elevator door opened. She entered and pushed the button for the lobby.

Their eyes met, hers blazing with defiance, his infinitely patient. "I'll call you," Roman said. "About our date," he tacked on when she appeared disinclined to answer.

The steel door closed. But not so quickly that he couldn't hear her muttered curse.

Feeling strangely lighthearted for the first time in weeks, Roman found himself looking forward to the most expensive date of his life.

SHE WAS A Saxon noblewoman. Pure of mind, body and spirit. Intelligent and utterly fearless. Her life had been perfect until William the Conqueror invaded her beloved island. Although she'd sworn never to pledge allegiance to these barbaric warriors, she'd been taken captive and forced to pledge a marriage vow to the hated Norman baron who'd taken her family's land.

After a ceremony attended by William himself, Brianna was sent by her new husband to the bedchamber and told to prepare for her wedding night. The night grew long. Then longer. Brianna could hear the sounds of merriment coming from the Great Hall as she awaited her husband's arrival.

The light was a pale stuttering silver when the heavy wooden door finally opened, rousing her from a light slumber.

"Well, wife." He stood there, filling the doorway. "I thought I gave instructions for you to wait my arrival."

"I *was* waiting, my lord." Her dulcet tone was edged with sarcasm. She'd be buried in the churchyard before this devil would ever be her lord.

"You were sleeping." His hands on his hips, he moved toward her, menace in his steely blue gaze.

She lifted her chin in an instinctively defiant gesture. "And you, sir, were tardy."

He lifted his hand, as if to strike her, but fisted his wide hand in her unbound hair instead. "A good Norman wife would never dare speak that way to her husband."

"If you'd wanted a good Norman wife, sir, you should have stayed at home and married one."

"God's blood, you are a mouthy wench." When he caressed her frowning lips with his thumb, she bit it. Hard.

His shouted oath, as he jerked his hand free, was even cruder than she would have expected from a barbarian. "Before tonight is over, wife," he roared, "you will learn to be a subservient, proper wife."

"I'd rather be dead." She tried to toss her head and flinched when he pulled her hair so hard she felt as if he was yanking it from the roots.

"That can be arranged." He took hold of her night-gown and with one mighty yank, ripped it down the center. "Later." His gaze took a slow tour of her body, lingering for an unnervingly long time on her breasts, which she refused to cover with her hands. "Much, much later."

He reached out and ran his rough hand over the sensual path his eyes had scorched, creating havoc to every one of her nerve endings. "Your mind may not have accepted the idea of our marriage, wife," he said in a husky voice. "But your body has. See what happens when I do this." Although she refused to look as instructed, when he caught the tingling bud between his thumb and forefinger, she felt it turn as hard as a pebble.

Her head was swimming. As she felt her legs weakening, Brianna struggled against fainting. "If you do this, I'll hate you."

"That does not come as any surprise." He ran his palm down her torso, over her stomach, then lower still. "The problem is, my reluctant Saxon bride, is that if I do not do this, I'll hate myself."

His fingers traced a flaming path through the cloud of soft, silky platinum hair. When he tugged on those pale curls, another shot of heat threatened to overwhelm her.

Without thinking, she slapped him.

The sudden, sharp sound was like the crack of a tree branch in the stillness of the bedchamber. He didn't flinch. But she could see the storm clouds building in his eyes.

"I should beat you."

She lowered her hand. "I'd rather be beaten to blood pudding than be raped."

"Perhaps I'll do both." He rubbed his bearded chin thoughtfully. "Beat you. Then rape you." He pushed the rendered white gown off her shoulders. It fell to the floor, *leaving her totally vulnerable to his dark, masculine scrutiny.*

"*You truly are a comely wench, wife,*" *he murmured, nodding with satisfaction.* "*I must remember to thank William in the morning.*"

If you are still alive. *Clinging to her fury, Brianna thought of the knife she'd hidden beneath the bed and felt some faint measure of comfort.*

"*If I kiss you, will you bite me? As you did my thumb?*" *he inquired in a remarkably even tone.*

"*I will spit in your face.*"

He sighed wearily. "*I was afraid of that.*" *He picked up the nightgown and tore a long strip off it.*

"*You'd dare gag me?*" *Forgetting her lack of clothing, she rose to her full height, every inch the royal born lady she was.*

"*A prudent knight knows the value of defensive maneuvers.*" *Before she could utter a word of complaint, he wrapped the white cloth around her head and over her mouth.* "*Though God's truth, it is a shame, not to be able to taste those succulent, ripe lips . . .*

"*Perhaps later.*" *He pressed his fingertips against the gag and, enraging her further, smiled as he tore another long strip from her bridal nightgown.* "*When I've properly tamed you.*"

He laughed a bold rich laugh at her expense as he scooped her up and carried her over to the bed, dropping her as if she were a stone.

When she tried to strike him, he caught both her wrists in his large dark hand, lashed them together with the white material and tied them to the bedpost. His eyes didn't move from hers as he took off his own clothes. Unable to curse him, bound like a pig on the way to market, Brianna fought back with the only weapon she had left in her arsenal. Her glare was hot enough to turn a lump of coal to ashes.

Unfortunately her husband was not a lump of coal, but a man. A very large, very aroused male.

He spread her legs apart and knelt between them, taking in the beads of moisture glistening like diamonds in those soft blond curls.

"I think you do not hate me as much as you say," he murmured, on a rough, deep voice that vibrated deep within her. "I believe, wife, that we will prove to be well matched."

She was wet and slick, but he was larger than she could have imagined. When she felt the moist tip of his rampant sex begin to invade her body, she tensed.

"That will only make things worse, wife." He reached between them and boldly cupped her most private place. "'Tis better when you relax."

There was no question this man was the devil. He knew just where to touch, how much pressure to exert. When those clever, wicked fingers stroked an ultrasensitive nub of flesh, lightning forked through her.

Sensing her surrender, he lifted her hips and drove inside her with one forceful, mighty stroke, filling her completely. Her cry of pain was muffled by the strip of cloth covering her mouth. Tears streamed down her pale cheeks. She tried to break free of her restraints, but he'd tied the knots too tightly.

Using his weight to hold her prisoner, he paused long enough to rip away the gag.

"Please, my lord." She was no longer too proud to beg. "Please stop this torture."

Something that could have been sympathy flashed in his stormy eyes. "'Tis too late to stop now, wife." He reached between them again and resumed stroking that tingling bit of pink flesh, creating a restlessness that had her unconsciously lifting her hips.

He covered her unbound mouth with his, treating her to a forceful kiss designed to stake his claim on her once and for all as he began to move again, driving her deeper and deeper into the feather mattress, his thrusts growing more forceful, more out of control.

She was trembling. Not from fear or anger, but from an escalating need for fulfillment. Having never felt like this in her life, she feared she would die from this primal pleasure he'd forced upon her.

Her body clutched brazenly at his as he drove them both into a heat so hot it could only be the flames of hell. She was crying out, begging him to end this tender torment, damning him for making her suffer so.

The first orgasm literally rocked her. But he refused to stop, demanding more and more. Amazingly, she climaxed again before he finally gave into his own release, flooding her throbbing, pulsating body with his seed.

HELL. This was a mistake, Roman decided, as he took a deep breath and closed the slender red book. Reading erotica while his body was still aching for its sexy author did nothing to quiet the hunger in him.

He'd discovered Desiree's secret by accident, during a rare visit to New York. His agent had been called into the reception area to deal with some mixup regarding an overnight package, leaving Roman alone. Impatient, and edgy, as he always was when forced to spend time in Manhattan, he began to roam the office.

And that's when he first saw the book, in the chrome out basket. A letter to Desiree Dupree was clipped to the cover.

It had read: "Dear Desiree, here's an advance copy of *Fears and Fantasies,* hot off the presses. This should certainly satisfy all those readers who wrote demanding more stories along the lines of *Scarlet Ribbons.* Congratulations."

Desiree had already piqued his interest during her appearances on the nightly news. As he'd skimmed through the volume of sensual stories, Roman had realized that the outwardly cool, competent crime reporter definitely possessed a great deal of hidden, turbulent waters.

When he'd questioned his agent about her, he'd received only a vague comment that due to her high-profile career, the author preferred to remain anonymous.

His agent's less than forthcoming attitude hadn't deterred Roman. He'd already decided to meet Desiree. The fact that she'd shown up on his doorstep at the worst possible time in his life proved that Fate did indeed move in mysterious ways.

A low ache of hunger twisted his gut into nasty, painful knots as he imagined himself drawn into the seductive scene Desiree had created.

"Damn." His body throbbing, his head pounding, Roman dragged his hand down his face, wondering when he'd become such a masochist. Then, although he knew it would only make the wanting worse, he opened the slender red book once more and continued to read.

WHITE LIGHTS HAD BEEN strung in the trees and on the arched gateways at New Orleans's Armstrong Park, transforming the area into a Christmas fairyland.

Sixteen-year-old Tabitha Sue Jackson was standing outside the lighted arch, dancing in place in a vain attempt to keep warm. It was hard enough perching on four-inch-high heels all night; the freezing temperatures not only made working hell, they kept the johns away. And when that happened...

No! She wasn't going to think about anything bad. Not this close to Christmas. After all, until this damn cold front had blown in, business had been booming. From the way her secret stash had been growing the past few nights, Tabitha concluded that this truly was the season of goodwill. She couldn't remember the last time she'd made so much money.

In another week she'd have enough to buy Christmas presents for all her sisters and brothers back in Boise and still be able to afford that fluffy white rabbit coat she'd seen in the window at Holmes Department Store on Canal. Damn, couldn't she use that coat tonight!

Trying to lift her spirits, she broke into a cheerful chorus of "Sleigh Ride," which always reminded her of the times, back before her parents had gotten divorced and her mother had remarried that creep Tabitha always thought of as Roger the Pervert, when the family would go out into the Idaho woods to cut their own Christmas tree.

Her mother would bring along sandwiches and a thermos of cocoa, and as they'd drive through the snow-covered forest, they'd sing Christmas songs. And although her younger brothers and sisters always confused the words to "Sleigh Ride" with the lyrics from "Winter Wonderland," no one had ever minded.

The memory, unlike so many others, was a good one, warming her from the inside out. As she danced in place, the silver bells she'd sewn on the hem of her short red miniskirt added a merry accompaniment to the Christmas tune. Her shiny black, thigh-high boots tapped a rhythm on the uneven stone sidewalk.

"'It's lovely weather,'" she sang in an enthusiastic, if slightly off-key, contralto, "'for a sleigh ride together—'" she pointed at a passing motorist who'd slowed to watch "'—with you!'"

On cue, the black Porsche came to a stop.

"All right!" She danced over to the car. When she reached the passenger door, the automatic window rolled down.

"Are you one of Santa's little elves?" the driver asked. His hooded eyes gleamed in the diffused glow of the streetlight. His lips were curved in a smile that revealed a row of strong, perfect white teeth.

Tabitha couldn't hold back her grin. She'd known the little red Santa's helper dress would prove to be a gold mine. This was definitely her lucky night. From the looks of the car, the guy was loaded. And he was a lot better looking than most of the creeps who trolled the Quarter for teenage girls.

He kind of reminded her of Richard Gere, which was a definite plus. Like most of the girls working New Orleans' streets, Tabitha fantasized about having some rich hunk in an imported sports car fall madly in love with her.

"It could happen," she'd insisted just this afternoon to her best friend and sometimes roommate, Jolene.

"And pigs will fly all over the Quarter," Jolene had snapped back. At twenty-five, she had given up on waiting for Prince Charming. "Better wear a hat tonight, girl. To protect your pretty blond head from all that pig shit."

Well, with any luck, tonight would be the night she proved Jolene wrong, Tabitha thought.

"I can be anyone you want me to be," she promised. Her breath came out in little, ghostlike white puffs. She flashed her most appealing smile and tossed her long blond hair back over her shoulder. The red-green-and-yellow lights in her battery-operated Christmas tree earrings flashed merrily. "Feel like a little Christmas cheer?"

"It *is* the season for parties." His dark eyes—either blue or black, Tabitha couldn't quite tell in the shadows cast from the streetlight—moved slowly over her face. "Have you been a good little girl?"

"Actually—" her cherry red lips turned down in a mock mew "—I'm afraid I've been a naughty little girl."

He flashed her another one of those Richard Gere smiles. "My favorite kind." He glanced with seeming impatience into his rearview mirror. "You'd think people would have enough sense to stay home on a night like this," he muttered at the steady stream of traffic.

"We can go to my place." The rented motel room a few doors down Rampart wasn't much, but it did have heat. Since she'd been standing still, the cold had caught up with her, making her teeth begin to chatter.

"I've got a better idea," he said. She heard the click of the passenger door unlocking. "Let's go to my place. You are available for the night?"

This was getting better and better. Feeling just like Julia Roberts, Tabitha grinned. "I'm all yours, sweetheart. For as long as you want." As she opened the door, a rush of warmth from the Porsche's heater welcomed her.

Jolene was wrong, Tabitha decided as she settled into the onyx leather bucket seat. There *was* a Santa Claus, after all.

6

ALTHOUGH SHE WAS exhausted by the time she finally fell into bed, Desiree only slept in snatches. And whenever she did manage to drift off, her dreams were filled with dizzying, confusing images of tombs, tangled gardens, jungle rain forests and thunderstorms. The scenes shifted, constantly tilting and changing like the facets of some dark-lensed kaleidoscope. The only thing that remained constant was that Roman Falconer played a starring role in each and every one.

She dreamed of him as she'd first seen him, his eyes dark and strangely haunted as he stood at the fringe of spectators crowding the sidewalk outside the cemetery. She pictured him in his library, looking at her with an edgy, reckless desire in his hypnotic eyes—the view of the overgrown garden in the background.

She dreamed about that kiss they'd shared, the simulated rainstorm swirling around them while another, more violent storm raged inside her, leaving her reeling and helpless. Helpless against the practiced seduction of his firm, hot mouth; helpless against her own answering need.

And then, heaven help her, as the hour grew later and the full moon rose higher, her dreams grew darker.

She was standing nude, save for a wide, gold, stone-studded belt that had been locked around her waist, in a Bedouin tent somewhere in the Arabian Desert, wrists chained in front of her as a dark-haired man dressed in a white, open-necked cotton shirt, jodphurs and tall leather boots slowly circled her.

"She appears suitable," he murmured.

"Oh, more than suitable," the turbaned slave vendor insisted. "The woman has been trained by experts in the erotic arts. She will do anything you desire. Without question."

The man's midnight eyes moved over her, from the top of her auburn head down to her toes, the nails of which had been painted a gleaming pearl white. There was a primitive, feral sexuality in his dark gaze. "Anything?" he asked at length.

"She is your sexual slave," the smaller man insisted.

The dark-haired man lifted his riding crop and trailed the thin black whip down her throat, across her breasts, following the spiraling lines of the hennaed nimbus that encircled her nipples. As he watched the rosy buds tighten at the potentially treacherous touch of leather, he smiled his satisfaction.

"I'll take her." His eyes, almost jet with passion and power, returned to hers. "My man will pay you."

"Thank you, sir. You will not be disappointed." Knowing when he was no longer welcome, the slave trader backed out of the tent.

"I do not plan to be." The dark-haired man's words, silky with menace, husky with sex, were directed at Desiree. With his hypnotizing eyes locked on hers, he placed his dark hand on her bare shoulder, silently commanding her to kneel.

He was the devil in the skin of a pagan god. Shivering with a complex blend of fear and wicked anticipation, Desiree had no choice but to obey her master.

When her clock radio came on, dragging her from her fitful sleep, Desiree's body was throbbing with unrequited need.

"This is ridiculous," she grumbled as she fought to free herself from the tangle of sheets. She had to stop thinking of Roman. She had to stop dreaming of him. She had to stop wanting him.

Even as she assured herself that she was not responsible for whatever scandalous and politically incorrect scenarios her rebellious, subconscious mind conjured up, Desiree vowed not to allow him to continue to infiltrate her thoughts.

She was behaving like a foolish schoolgirl, getting all emotional over a man who seduced, then discarded women like plastic Mardi Gras doubloons. Oh, he may have turned reclusive lately, but there had been a time, not so long ago, when Roman Falconer had been socially and romantically linked with too many women in town.

By the time she'd showered and dressed for work, Desiree had sworn yet again that she was not going to succumb to Roman's admittedly considerable charms.

WSLU-TV was located on Rue de Royal, the street where, once upon a time, the Streetcar Named Desire ran. Home of three of the city's most important banks in the 1800s, the French Quarter street was now known for its expensive antique shops.

Desiree had always enjoyed working in the Vieux Carre. Until today, when she realized that she was little more than a stone's throw away from Roman's home.

The newsroom was, as always, chaotic. Cardboard coffee cups littered desktops, phones rang constantly, people hunkered over computer keyboards, tapping madly away. Perched atop a ladder in the corner of the room, Matthew Raynes, former quarterback for LSU turned sports reporter, flirted with the blond weather forecaster who'd arrived last week from KTSP in Phoenix and who was instructing him on the placement of lights on a fragrant pine tree. Observing them, Desiree envied their carefree banter.

She hadn't been involved with a man since her breakup with Michael months ago. It wasn't that she was carrying a torch. Or harboring a grudge. She simply hadn't met any other man who interested her nearly as much as her work.

Until yesterday, she amended as she poured herself a cup of coffee. Until Roman Falconer.

The truth of the matter, as much as she'd love to deny it, even to herself, was that he fascinated her. Too much for comfort.

Although a headache was pounding behind her eyes, Desiree welcomed the near bedlam that came with frantic daily deadlines. It helped take her mind off the man who'd already infiltrated too many of her waking and sleeping hours.

She'd barely sat down at her desk to go through her mail when a delivery boy arrived with a long white box tied with a scarlet satin ribbon.

So much for forgetting about Roman, Desiree thought with an inward sigh as she tipped the delivery boy and untied the ribbon. Personally she found long-stemmed flowers excessive coming from a man she'd just met, but she couldn't deny that the shared kiss had definitely speeded up their timetable.

She couldn't find a card in the dark greenery, but Desiree had no doubt that the long-stemmed roses were from Roman. Even the color—a deep crimson so dark as to be nearly black—reminded her of the enigmatic writer. The blossoms were full-blown, their sweet scent almost overwhelming.

As she drew one rose from the box, a thorn stabbed her flesh, leaving a pinpoint of bright red blood on her fingertip.

Tossing the blossom back in with the others, she took the box into the ladies room and dumped it into the wastebasket.

"What are you doing?" Karyn Collins, the producer of the station's early morning and noon newscasts, protested. "Don't tell me O'Malley's trying to get things started again?"

"Roses aren't O'Malley's style," Desiree said. Her wounded finger stung and began to bleed again. Turning on the tap, she stuck it beneath a stream of cold water. "And for the record, Michael and I are just friends."

"I'm glad to hear that," Karyn said quickly. Too quickly, Desiree thought, looking at her colleague with renewed interest. As the producer blushed, realization dawned.

"I hadn't realized you and Michael were an item."

"We're not." Once again Karyn's answer came a bit too swiftly. "At least, not like the two of you were. Right now we're just kind of taking things day by day."

"That's probably best."

Karyn's worried dark eyes met Desiree's in the mirror. "Are you certain you don't mind? I only started going out with him because he assured me it was over between the two of you."

"It is."

Desiree felt only honest pleasure that Michael was involved with a woman as nice as Karyn. The divorced mother of two had not had an easy time, balancing work with her maternal duties. From what Desiree had been able to tell, she hadn't had any social life at all for quite a while. Until now.

"Michael's a great guy," she said. "I hope things work out for you both."

Casting one last disparaging glance at the roses scattered among the discarded paper towels, Desiree returned to her desk and picked up the telephone receiver.

Roman answered on the first ring. "Hello?" His tone was brusque, leaving Desiree to wonder if she'd interrupted him while he was writing. *Tough*.

"This is Desiree Dupree—" she began in the same brisk, professional voice she would have used were she calling the mayor to verify a quote.

"Ms. Dupree." Even as he cut off her planned complaint, his voice warmed, irritating Desiree even further. If he thought she was just another one of his fall-into-bed-at-the-pop-of-a-champagne-cork socialites, he had another think coming. "Tell me you're calling to set the time for our date."

"Actually, I'm calling about the flowers. I realize you must have spent a great deal of money, but—"

"What flowers?"

"The roses."

"Roses?"

She was usually very good at detecting nuances in a person's voice—her job depended on it. And although it didn't make any sense, Desiree would have bet her Emmy that Roman Falconer was not faking his confusion.

"Are you saying you didn't send me two dozen roses this morning?"

"That's precisely what I'm saying. Coincidentally, I considered it," he added as an afterthought. "But I decided it might be overkill. Considering we haven't even had our first official date. Yet," he tacked on in a sexy drawl that strummed unbidden, unwelcome chords inside Desiree.

"You're right. It would be excessive," she agreed, even as she tried to think of someone else who might be prone to behave so extravagantly. "But if it wasn't you . . ." Her voice drifted off.

"Sounds as if you've got a secret admirer," Roman suggested. "Which shouldn't come as that much of a surprise, considering that you're intelligent, sexy and highly visible. Surely this isn't the first time you've received flowers from a fan."

"No. But they usually send a card."

"Perhaps the florist forgot to include it."

It was, of course, the logical answer. But somehow Desiree didn't think it was all that simple. She glanced down at her finger, which still stung, remembered that scarlet drop of blood and could not quite shake the lingering feeling that the dark red roses were in some way evil.

"I'm sure that must be it," she agreed. "I'm sorry to have bothered you."

"You could never be a bother, Desiree." His already deep voice dipped enticingly into its lowest register. "Let me know when you're ready for our date."

"I will." She wondered what he'd say if she suggested New Year's Eve in the year 2001.

"It would also be nice if it could be in this century."

The man was dangerous enough without adding mind-reading skills to his repertoire. Desiree decided it was time to bring this conversation to a close. "Goodbye, Mr. Falconer."

"Roman," he reminded her. "Oh, and Desiree?"

"Yes?"

"If you change your mind about wanting flowers, just let me know."

Irritated by the masculine confidence in his tone, she hung up without responding.

A call to the florist offered no explanation. The roses had been paid for, in cash, by a dark-haired man who hadn't wanted to enclose a card. A secret admirer, as Roman had suggested.

Given, as he'd also pointed out, her high visibility, it was not an impossible idea. So why did it make her feel threatened?

Because of last year's stalker, she admitted to herself.

Determined to put the mystery out of her mind for now, she resumed opening her mail.

Several of the letters stacked in her In basket were in response to a story she'd done on attempts to curtail prostitution in Armstrong Park. Another particularly strident letter suggested she do an exposé about the inability to locate decent citizen parking at the city courthouse center. There were also the usual requests asking her to appear at charity events or to speak to local civic and school groups.

Three of the letters were marked Personal. One was from a seven-year-old boy, inviting her to marry his widowed father. She put that one aside, intending to send a polite refusal that would somehow discourage the young boy without hurting his feelings.

The second, written in pencil on a legal pad, was a rambling discourse from a man professing to have been her husband in another life—in eighteenth-century London. Having already dealt with one obsessed fan, and wondering if this could be the man who'd sent the roses, she put that letter aside as well. Michael had handled her stalker case, and she intended to pass it on to him—just in case.

The third one, typewritten on expensive, linen bond paper, made her blood run cold.

"Desiree?" Karyn paused on her way by the desk. Her dark eyes revealed concern. "Are you all right?"

"I don't know." Desiree stared at the type, which seemed to be swimming on the page. "He says I'm the only one he can trust to tell his story."

"Don't tell me it's another one of those UFO crack-pots."

"No." Desiree carefully put the paper down on her desk and pressed one of the autodial buttons on her phone. "It's the rapist. He's unhappy about the lack of press he's been getting."

"You're joking!"

"It's not exactly a joking matter. He also says he hoped I enjoyed the roses."

"Those roses were from the rapist?" Karyn's lips turned down in an appropriate frown, but Desiree recognized the glint of excitement in the producer's expressive eyes.

"You'd better dust off your mantel," she said as Desiree waited for the operator at the downtown police complex to answer the phone. "Because this is definitely Emmy-winning material. When news breaks that the French Quarter rapist is writing you love letters—"

"It's not a love letter."

"Okay, a fan letter, whatever. But when the word gets out, you'll probably get offers from the networks—*60 Minutes, 20/20,* maybe even *Nightline.* Make me one promise."

"If I can." Growing more and more impatient, Desiree was tempted to hang up and dial 911 since no one was picking up the damn phone.

"When you go on *Nightline*, put in a good word with Koppel for me? I'd love to go network."

As appalling as she found the prospect of becoming part of the story she was covering, Desiree could not deny that the idea of appearing on *Nightline*, and getting to talk on the air with Ted Koppel, was more than a little appealing.

"Hello?" she said when a voice on the other end of the line finally answered. "This is Desiree Dupree from WSLU-TV, calling Detective O'Malley regarding the recent French Quarter rapes."

She listened, frustrated, as the voice on the other end of the line began to give her the official "no comment" line.

"Yes, I realize he's busy on a case," she said, interrupting the desk sergeant, "but I think he'll talk to me. I'm not looking for a ten-second sound bite for the six o'clock news. Tell him the rapist he's trying to apprehend wants to arrange a meeting."

Desiree was not surprised when the detective made it to the phone in record time. He'd told her to stay put and he'd come to her.

She was waiting at her desk, staring with dark dread at the florist's box she'd retrieved from the ladies room, when she heard his deep, familiar voice across the room. Glancing up, she noticed he'd stopped by Karyn's desk.

They might just be taking it day by day, but they were obviously both more involved than Karyn, at least, was willing to admit. Although their expressions were schooled to make it appear they were simply having a casual conversation, there was no mistaking the private messages their eyes were exchanging.

Although it hurt her pride to admit it, Michael O'Malley had never, in all their time together, looked at her the way he was looking at Karyn. Nor had she, Desiree decided honestly, looked at Michael with nearly as much intensity and hunger.

Sensual tension surrounded the couple like a field force until, strangely embarrassed, Desiree dragged her gaze away and pretended interest in the newest stack of memos sent down from the lofty echelons of station management.

"Is this them?"

Desiree turned her attention from the memos and looked a long way up into O'Malley's ruggedly handsome face.

He'd dispensed with polite formalities—like saying hello—which wasn't that surprising, since he'd reverted to the Joe Friday, just-the-facts-ma'am mode he tended to fall into whenever he was working on an important case. She'd seen it happen too many times to take offense.

"Yes," she said, understanding that he was referring to the flowers that took up a major portion of her desk. "I'm afraid I probably got my fingerprints all over the box."

He shrugged. "It doesn't matter. Since it came from the florist, I doubt if the guy even touched it."

He rubbed his chin as he studied the flowers. "Aren't roses usually sent out as buds?"

"That's usually the case."

"Is there a card?"

"No. In fact, at first I thought they were from . . ." She paused, strangely unwilling to bring Roman Falconer into the investigation.

"From who?" he prompted.

"No one." It was her turn to shrug. "I have a high profile in the community. Sometimes strange men send me flowers."

"Strange men like your stalker."

"Yes." As they exchanged a long glance fraught with memories, she knew they were both thinking the same thing. She'd met Michael when he'd shown up at the station to investigate her case. Thanks to him, the man in question was currently serving time in the Louisiana State Prison.

Although O'Malley's behavior had been nothing short of professional during the investigation, it would have been impossible to ignore their shared, mutual attraction. The night her tormentor was finally behind bars, Detective First Class Michael Patrick O'Malley and Desiree had become lovers.

"I called the florist," she said, returning to his reason for coming to the station, "to see if he could tell me who'd sent them. But the man paid cash."

"I'll drop by and see if I can get a description." His gaze slid from her face to the roses again. "He must have arranged to buy them open like that. Which means the florist would have to hold them for a few days."

"I suppose so, unless the delivery boy wasn't really from the florist." Her blood instantly ran cold as another, chilling thought occurred to her. "Oh, my God. You don't think he could have been the one, do you?"

"It's hard to say. But just in case, I'll want you to meet with a police artist. Along with anyone else here who saw the guy."

"Fine." Desiree nodded, wishing she'd paid more attention to the young delivery man.

"Where's the letter?"

"Right there." She pointed to it, not wanting to touch it again.

He skimmed the lines, cursed under his breath, then, holding the paper by the edges, slipped it into a glassine bag, which he labeled, then stuck in his jacket pocket. He scooped up the flower box. "Let's go."

"Where?"

"I don't know. Maybe we'll just drive around the city and talk about this guy."

"Why can't we talk here?"

"In a television newsroom?" His tone suggested that he'd rather attempt to discuss the case on Bourbon Street on Fat Tuesday. "As impossible as it's probably going to turn out to be, I'm trying to maintain a low profile on this case."

"So you said. And I still don't agree with that tactic."

"What else is new? We've never agreed on much of anything," he reminded her. He plucked her purse from the desktop and held it out to her. "Let's go."

There had been a time when being ordered around by this man would have made her see red. When she realized that his autocratic behavior no longer irritated her, she took that as proof positive that things really were over between them.

"I love it when you pull out that macho, me-Tarzan, you-Jane act, O'Malley," she said in dulcet tones. Bestowing her sweetest, most-feigned smile on him, she took her purse and walked out of the newsroom, leaving him to follow.

Which he did. But not before, Desiree noticed, stopping to exchange another brief word with Karyn.

"You realize, of course, that she's going to want to put this on the air," Desiree said five minutes later as the car inched its way through the holiday tourists crowding the

Quarter. The same tourists, she reminded herself, that the city council was so concerned about frightening away.

"Who?" he asked, slanting her a glance as he waited for a red light at Canal Street.

"Karyn." She waited a beat. "In case you've forgotten, she *is* a news producer. And when a serial rapist sends flowers and a letter to a reporter, like it or not, that's news."

He stared straight ahead as he pondered that. But watching the way his fingers tightened on the steering wheel, Desiree suspected he'd not yet seen Karyn in a professional light. Originally from Georgia, the producer was the quintessential southern belle—soft as spun sugar on the outside, hardened steel within.

"I don't want this to get out. Not yet," he said at last.

"Is this the mayor talking? Or Detective First Class Michael O'Malley?"

There was, Desiree decided, a difference. If she was being asked to withhold a story for political reasons, the mayor and the rest of the city council could kiss her Emmy.

If, on the other hand, O'Malley was worried about her blowing his case, she'd be willing to listen.

The light changed. When the driver of the car behind them blared its horn, he cursed. "Let's wait until we get somewhere we can talk," he suggested. "Without worrying about traffic."

Since the day had dawned bright and balmy, after stopping at a convenience store for two cups of coffee, O'Malley drove to Audubon Park. The sprawling expanse of green, which extended all the way to the river, had once belonged to Bienville, the founder of New Orleans.

Many of the huge oak trees went back two centuries, to when the land had been part of the plantation where sugar had been granulated for the first time, in 1794. The spreading black limbs turned walkways into covered alleys, which wandered around peaceful, winding lagoons, fountains and statuary, including a bronze statue of John James Audubon, after whom the park was named. Entering the leafy environs, Desiree and O'Malley settled down on a bench in a white gazebo overlooking Whooping Crane Pond.

The December sun was warm, drawing students from Tulane and Loyola universities across St. Charles Avenue, some of whom turned the lawns into study halls, while others rode rented bikes and horses along the tree-lined paths.

Desiree and O'Malley remained silent for a moment, sipping coffee, watching a family of ducks on the small, man-made pond. Although she was admittedly impatient, once again Desiree waited, knowing the detective's penchant for choosing his words carefully.

"Yesterday, at breakfast," he said finally, "I was giving you the official party line."

"Jeez. What a surprise."

He shook his head in frustration. "You know, I'd almost forgotten how sarcastic you can be."

"To know me is to love me," she retorted with a grin. "As for you spouting the mayor's spin on the crime, I figured that out for myself."

"Beauty and brains," he drawled. "If you weren't such a smart ass, I probably would have married you."

"As I recall, it was me who didn't want to get married," she countered. Actually, at the time, neither one of them had been eager to make a run for the altar. "So why don't you just fill me in on our killer and save the sweet talk for Karyn?"

He shot her a surprised glance. "Is it that obvious?"

"Only about as obvious as the nose on that ruggedly handsome Irish mug of yours." Watching the embarrassed red flush rise from his white shirt collar, and knowing how he hated discussing personal feelings, Desiree took pity on him. "I'm happy for you, Mike." She put a hand on his arm. "Truly."

He expelled a relieved breath. "I told Karyn not to worry. That you wouldn't be upset if you found out we were seeing each other." He shook his head again. "But you know women. Always making an emotional issue of everything." As he realized what he'd just said, he began to backtrack. "Not that you...what I meant was..."

In spite of the gravity of the situation, Desiree laughed. "Point taken. And I think I'll accept what you were trying to say as a compliment and let it go at that. So, tell me why I can't open tonight's newscast with my obvious lead story."

"Because you're more involved than you think. And I don't want to risk you getting hurt."

"Don't you think that's being a bit overprotective? Despite the flowers, I don't think the guy's thinking of me as a woman, but rather as a reporter. A reporter who can make him a star."

"I would have agreed. Until the flowers."

"What about the flowers?" Other than the fact that for some reason she could not discern, they'd made her skin crawl even before she'd known they were from the rapist.

"They're the same kind he gives his victims. Afterward." His eyes darkened with a fury she'd only witnessed once before—after he'd arrested a prominent businessman for impregnating his own thirteen-year-old daughter. "But he isn't as generous with them. They only get a single rose. A single full-blown, bloodred rose."

An icy chill ran up her spine, then down again. "Perhaps, in some insane way, he simply thought two dozen roses might make me more inclined to tell his story," she suggested, the rationalization sounding feeble even to her own ears.

"I might be willing to buy that. Except for the other thing."

She was almost afraid to ask. "What other thing?"

"The reason we know it's the same guy is because he's got the same M.O."

"The roses."

"The roses." He nodded. "And the fact that he ties the girls up."

"Surely that's not so unusual. In rape cases."

"No. But it's what he uses to do it with."

A feeling of impending doom swept over Desiree, reminding her of a time when she'd been eleven, and she and a girlfriend had gone to a Halloween haunted house put on by the New Orleans Jaycees. Although she'd put on a brave front, secretly she'd been terrified as she made her way through the narrow, dark hallways, knowing that at any moment some monster was going to leap at her from the shadows.

That was the same way she felt now.

"Tell me it's a normal piece of clothesline."

He enclosed both her hands in his. "He uses silk ribbons, Desiree. Scarlet ribbons. The same kind used on the florist box. The same kind—"

"I used in my story."

Although the sun continued to shine overhead, Desiree felt as if a dark cloud had suddenly turned the sky ominously black.

And on the warmest December day on record, she suddenly began to shiver.

7

"YOU CAN'T POSSIBLY THINK that he knows..." Her words clogged in her throat. No. The idea was unimaginable.

"That you wrote those sex books?" O'Malley finished for her. His expression was as grim as she'd ever seen it. His eyes were hard, his jaw jutted out and deep lines bracketed his unsmiling lips.

"Erotica," she corrected automatically, her voice sounding as if it were coming from far, far away. Like from the bottom of the river. "Have I mentioned that I hate it when you refer to them as 'sex books'?"

"Call them what you like, you can't deny that they glamorize rape."

They'd had this argument more times than Desiree cared to count. O'Malley was one of the very few people who knew she was the author of those slender volumes of erotica. She'd been working on one during the brief time they'd been living together, and it would have been impossible to keep her secret from any lover, let alone a skilled detective.

"My books don't glamorize rape any more than those murder mysteries you eat up like popcorn glamorize serial killing," she countered. Caught up in the familiar argument, she momentarily forgot the dread that had swept over her when she'd heard about the scarlet ribbons. "As a writer, I try to get a reader to suspend disbelief. To lose herself in a story."

"A story about one of the most brutal acts committed against women."

"In real life, that's true." She would willingly grant him that point. "But I don't write about real life, O'Malley. *Scarlet Ribbons* was pure fantasy."

"Try telling that to the rapist who sent you those flowers."

He definitely had her there. Desiree felt her argument collapsing like a pricked balloon.

"Point taken." She rubbed her temples. As she looked up at him, a vulnerability she seldom allowed to surface showed in her worried eyes. "It has to be a coincidence." She forced herself to remain calm. To think.

"How many people know you wrote those books?" he asked.

"There's you, of course. And my agent. And my editor. And Jan, in the contracts department." She dragged a hand through her hair as she thought the matter over.

"I suppose there's a possibility that my editor may have let something slip in-house, but she realizes that it could damage my reporting career, so I doubt she'd make such a mistake."

"What about the bank? Obviously you cash checks from the publisher."

"The publishing house writes a check to my agent. Who then takes out his ten percent and writes me a check—under my pseudonym—for the remainder. Which I deposit by mail."

"In a local bank?"

"Actually, no. I've set up an account under my pseudonym in a bank in the Grand Caymans."

"Are you telling me that you're laundering the money in some off-shore bank?" His tone, and his expression, were incredulous.

"I'm not laundering anything," she insisted on a huff of frustrated breath.

It was times like this, when they'd start arguing over anything and everything, that she remembered why they were no longer together.

"I'm just trying to keep my anonymity. And off-shore banks aren't nearly so picky about knowing exactly who they're dealing with."

"For good reason," he muttered disgustedly, "since most of their clients are crooks." His own frustration showing, he rubbed his square jaw thoughtfully. "So what you're saying is that it's highly unlikely that anyone in New Orleans knows you're the writer of sex— okay, novels of erotica," he corrected at her sharp look.

She opened her mouth to answer when, once again, Roman came to mind. Although she'd been surprised to find her books in his personal library, at the time she'd convinced herself it was merely a coincidence.

Now she couldn't help but wonder.

"Desiree?" O'Malley prompted.

No. She shook her head. The mystery writer might be a little unorthodox, but what writer wasn't? He might have a few rough edges, but so did a lot of men. And the fact that he was the kind of dark and dangerous male who made her feel both vulnerable and excited at the same time, and all too aware of being a woman, did not mean that he spent his nights roaming the French Quarter, like some twentieth-century Jack the Ripper, preying on helpless women.

"I'm sorry." She schooled her expression to one of calmness. "I was thinking about what whoever sent those flowers might want from me."

"I'd say that's pretty obvious."

"Is it?" She considered that a moment. "You don't really think it has something to do with my books?"

"I know damn well it does," he growled, frustration rearing its ugly head again. "Do you still have that .25 I gave you?"

He'd given her the gun when she was being stalked. He'd also taken her to the police range and taught her how to shoot it. And although it had made her uneasy, she couldn't deny that the blue-steel pistol had provided a certain sense of security.

"It's in the bottom drawer of my dresser, beneath some sweatshirts. I try not to think about it."

"You might want to move it to the top drawer."

"Surely you don't believe—"

"Dammit, Desiree, the guy uses the same ribbons you wrote into your book."

"I'm willing to concede that's a remarkable coincidence. Not that he uses the ribbons, but that of all the reporters in town, he picked me to send the flowers to. But I still believe it's only a lucky fluke on his part. He probably doesn't even understand the significance of what he's done."

"I wish to hell I could believe that."

"You could if you weren't always looking at the dark side of life."

"It's my job to look at the dark side," he reminded her. "To go where the good people of New Orleans don't want to go. And to deal with the kind of garbage taxpayers want carted away."

Like her stalker. Once again, Desiree had to concede that he had a point. And for not the first time, she wondered how he found the strength to remain in such a demanding, depressing job day after day.

"The taxpayers definitely got their money's worth when you joined the force, O'Malley." Her hand was still nestled inside his large, strong one. She linked their fingers together and gave him a warm and genuine smile. "I told Karyn that you're one of the good guys."

"You were talking about me? With Karyn?" For a man who'd faced down more than his share of armed perpetrators, the absolute terror in the detective's voice was almost laughable.

"Just girl talk, O'Malley." She patted his cheek.

"Girl talk." He leaned his head back against a pillar and briefly closed his eyes. "I'm undoubtedly doomed."

"Not a chance. Unless every instinct I've got has gone on the blink, the lady's as hooked on you as you are on her."

His eyes popped open and he gave her a glance that was more than a little self-conscious. "Do you think so?"

"Absolutely."

He considered that for a long moment, then shrugged, as if putting the matter of his romantic life behind him for more important subjects.

"So here's the plan," he said, his tone revealing that he'd fallen back into his cop mode. "You're not going to have anything to do with this guy. I don't care if he sends you enough flowers to build a freaking Rose Bowl float. I don't care if he writes you letters every day, ties them with red satin ribbons and seals them with a kiss. You're to pretend you've never heard of him."

"That's ridiculous!"

"What's ridiculous is the idea of a reporter—a *female* reporter—getting chummy with some sicko who reads rape fantasies in novels, then gets off on reenacting them in real life."

"There was no *real* violence in any of my stories." Desiree felt obliged to defend her work yet again. "In each case, the theme of the tale is the heroine getting a fantasy man to do what she wants, while outwardly seeming to be forced to do what he wants. Being at the mercy of a physical force so much stronger than the heroine herself allows her—and the reader—to remain blameless for her most secret, politically incorrect desires."

"Dammit, I'm not going to sit here and argue political correctness with you, Desiree!" he exploded. "I'm not going to argue about this point, period. Not while a serial rapist is running around loose. You're not to have anything to do with the guy."

"Are you speaking as a friend or a cop?"

"Both." He spat out the single word from between clenched teeth. "As a friend—and a man who once loved you—I refuse to accept the idea of you being in danger."

"And as a cop?"

"I won't let you screw up my investigation."

"Ah." She nodded. "Now we're getting to the gist of the matter."

"Dammit, Desiree!"

He jumped to his feet and glared down at her. In the past, whenever they got to this point, the arguments would escalate until one of them—or both—would lose control. Fury would usually be followed in quick succession by passion, which inevitably led to lovemaking that was every bit as stormy as their fights.

There had been a time, not so long ago, when Desiree had believed that they might have made it, if they could have only stayed in bed twenty-four hours a day.

O'Malley took hold of her shoulders, his long fingers digging into the flesh beneath her sweater. "This isn't a fantasy. It isn't make believe. This guy's all too real. And he's dangerous. I don't want you getting involved."

"But I am involved. And if I ignore him, what's to stop him from going out and getting rid of his anger by raping some other unsuspecting woman?" If that happened, Desiree knew she'd never be able to forgive herself.

"He's already raping unsuspecting women," O'Malley reminded her succinctly. "He doesn't seem to need any additional motivation."

"What if I agree to meet with him?" The thought had been growing in the back of her mind since she'd first read the note that had accompanied the roses.

"Are you crazy?"

"You could use me as bait." She decided against mentioning that she'd seen just such a plot device lots of times in the movies.

Desiree's journalistic instincts were humming. Talk about a scoop! Nabbing the French Quarter rapist and saving the city's Mardi Gras would not only make the mayor and city council very happy, it could well earn her a coveted spot at the network.

"Like hell I will!" There was a wild flurry of wings as O'Malley's explosive response caused the ducks gliding on the blue-green waters of Whooping Crane pond to take to the sky.

The two of them stood there, him glaring down at her, her looking defiantly back at him, until finally O'Malley proved he could still surprise her.

"You know," he murmured, "as much as I hate to admit it, that's not such a bad idea."

"Really?" The possibility of going undercover to catch a rapist had her feeling a lot like Wonder Woman.

"Really." He got that familiar, faraway look in his eyes that told Desiree he was working out a plan. "First, I want you to withhold the story. So he'll think you're ignoring him," he added, when she opened her mouth to argue.

"Oh. That's a good idea. It should make him frustrated and angry enough to make a mistake."

"Let's hope. We'll tap your phone at home. And your extension at work. Then, when the creep contacts you again, try to set up a meeting."

"I'll convince him to meet with me somehow." Excitement pulsed through her veins.

"You're not meeting anyone."

"But—"

"We'll have an undercover policewoman impersonate you, then we'll nab the sicko son-of-a-bitch."

So much for Wonder Woman. Knowing when she was outgunned, Desiree decided she should at least hold out for Lois Lane. "I don't like sharing center stage, but I suppose I don't have any choice." She shrugged and reminded herself that she still knew more about this case than any other reporter in town. "I'll make you a deal."

"You're not in any position to negotiate," he reminded her. "But I'm willing to listen."

"I'll agree to keep the story off the air. For now. But I get an exclusive when the guy's arrested."

He swore, but without heat. "Sold."

He tossed their empty cardboard coffee cups into a nearby trash can. As they walked back to the unmarked police car, Desiree was so caught up in the excitement of the moment that she failed to see the man, clad in black jeans and a black cashmere sweater, who was watching her intently from the shadows of an ancient oak tree.

ROMAN WAS SLOUCHED in a chair in the library of his allegedly haunted home, staring unseeingly out at the tangle that had once been a lovely Southern garden. Beside the French doors, Desiree's book *Private Passions* lay on the faded oriental carpet where it had landed when he'd thrown it across the room. Ironically, it had landed open to the short story he'd read all night long. Over and over again. As he had for the past three days, ever since Desiree Dupree had first shown up at his door.

Myriad erotic images from the book kept flashing in front of his mind's eye, like the seemingly never-ending mirrors in a carnival fun house. Images of women tied with red satin ribbons. Images of Desiree Dupree dressed in lacy lingerie, in black leather, in a short-skirted, white-fur-trimmed Santa's helper dress.

None of these dark fantasies would have been all that disturbing were it not for one fatal image that kept popping up in those endless mirrors, like a devilish joker in Mephistopheles's private deck of cards.

A reflection of himself. Dressed all in black. With blood on his hands.

Cursing, Roman dragged himself out of the chair and poured another glass of brandy from the new bottle he'd opened sometime during the long and sleepless night. Although it was not normal behavior for him to be drinking before noon, these were far from normal days.

The phone rang. And rang. As it had been doing for days.

Cradling the snifter in his hands, he listened as the answering machine picked up, expecting to hear his agent's voice inquiring where the hell he was and why he wasn't returning his calls. There was a movie deal on the table for *Killing Her Softly*. It was irresponsible, not to mention crazy, to turn incommunicado when so much money was at stake, the frustrated male voice had pointed out time and time again.

Roman took a long swallow of the brandy, prepared to ignore the call as he had all the others. But then the voice that had been haunting both his waking and sleeping hours came over the answering machine.

"Hello, Mr. Falconer?" Desiree's polite tone was far from intimate. Nevertheless, it stirred him in ways he didn't want to be stirred. "This is Desiree Dupree." As if he wouldn't recognize that throaty voice in the dark. Lord help him, *especially* in the dark.

There was a slight pause, as if she sensed he was standing there listening, and she was waiting for him to pick up. *Not on a bet, sweetheart.*

During these long, grueling, semidrunken hours of introspection, he'd decided that getting anywhere near the woman would be too damn dangerous.

Dangerous for him.

And more to the point, dangerous for *her.*

His fingers tightened on the stem of the glass.

"I was calling about that date you paid for. Since I'm not one to welsh on a deal, especially when it's for a good cause, I thought perhaps, if you weren't doing anything tonight . . . well, as it happens, I'm free."

She paused again. Utilizing every ounce of his willpower, Roman refrained from scooping up the receiver. "If you'd like, that is."

Another pause, a bit longer than the first. Roman pictured her combing her hand through her thick hair in frustration. And, he sensed, a bit of self-consciousness she was not accustomed to experiencing.

"Of course, if you'd like to just call the entire thing off, that's fine with me."

This time when she paused he caught the faint murmur of a curse so colorful it almost made him smile. Almost.

"It's just that you seemed so determined, I expected to hear from you. And when you didn't call, I thought . . ."

Another curse, a bit louder and even more pungent than the first. This time Roman felt his lips lift into a stiff half smile. Funny, after the other night he wouldn't have thought he'd ever have anything to smile about again.

Life, he decided was filled with surprises. Most of them these days were bad. As for Desiree, the jury was still out on her.

"Oh, hell, Falconer. If you want to go out, give me a call. If not, that's fine with me. I'm not going to sit around waiting by the phone like all your other women."

After she'd slammed the receiver down, he crossed the room to the machine, rewound the tape, then pressed play.

As her inimitable voice curled around him once again, Roman sipped his brandy and reminded himself that any involvement would be a mistake.

A mistake bound to prove as fatal as it was inevitable.

He heard a crack. Glancing down, he realized that the stem of the snifter had snapped, spilling brandy over his hand and down the front of his black jeans. He'd never realized the stems were that fragile.

As he watched the crimson blood begin to flow from the cut on his finger, Roman decided there must have been a flaw in the crystal.

DAMN THE MAN! Three days after her unsettling talk with O'Malley in Audubon Park, Desiree was tapping furiously away at her keyboard, turning her notes from an interview with a murderer on death row into a lead story.

Although the station had several competent, well-paid writers on staff, she'd never wanted to be just another pretty face who stood in front of the camera like a well-dressed ventriloquist's dummy and mouthed words someone else had written.

"You'd better be careful," Karyn said, pausing at her desk on the way to the editing room. "You pound on those poor keys any harder and you're going to have to go on the air with a broken fingernail."

"And wouldn't that be a tragedy," Desiree muttered, not taking her eyes from the screen. "Probably cost us at least five points in the ratings."

"At least," Karyn said good-naturedly. "Want to talk about it?"

"There's nothing to talk about." She skimmed the story, satisfied that she'd caught the essence of the man in his final interview. The pictures Sugar had taken would supply the visual punch.

"Whenever a woman says that she's furious about nothing, it's usually a man." Karyn pushed aside a stack of memos and perched a hip on the corner of the desk. "Something going wrong with your love life?"

"What love life?" Desiree muttered as she hit the Save key with unnecessary force.

"Ah." Karyn nodded. "I'm sorry."

"Oh, hell." Fearing that Karyn was apologizing for having fallen in love with Michael, Desiree dragged her eyes from the screen and leaned back in her chair, willing her body and mind to relax.

"I'm being a bitch. I know it. And believe me, I couldn't be happier about you and O'Malley. Perhaps I am a little envious," she admitted. "Of what the two of you have together. But it was never like that with Mike and me, Karyn. And it never would have been. We're too different."

"Actually," Karyn mused, "I think the problem might have been that you're too much alike."

"How on earth did you come to that conclusion?"

"You can't deny that you both have an overwhelming need to be right. All of the time."

"So what's wrong with being right?"

She laughed. "Thanks for proving my point." Her smile faded as she studied Desiree's drawn face. "It's the rapist, isn't it?" she suggested.

"Yes and no. I can't figure out what he's up to. Why would he send me flowers and write a note complaining about not getting any press, then, when I still don't say a word about him on the air, not even bother to respond?"

She glared over at the phone, which the police had tapped, willing it to ring. It wasn't as if she really wanted to talk to the rapist, but the waiting was driving her crazy. And then there was the little matter of Roman Falconer. . . .

No! She was not going to think about the temperamental, enigmatic mystery writer.

"Perhaps he got mad and left town," Karyn suggested, bringing her mind back to the other man who was never completely out of her thoughts these days. "Or maybe he's dead."

"Dead? Why on earth would he be dead?"

"Hey, even serial rapists must have heart attacks. Or get run over by a taxi, which in this town is more likely."

"One can only hope," Desiree muttered. The headache she'd woken up with this morning was coming back. She reached into a drawer, poured two aspirins from a plastic bottle and swallowed them with a drink of cold coffee. "But I can't quite shake the feeling that he's still out there. Waiting."

"For what?"

"That," Desiree said, putting her cup down with a snap, "is the $64,000 question."

THIS HAD TO STOP, dammit! Roman pointed the remote-control device at the television, darkening the screen. He needed Desiree Dupree in his life like he needed more of those damn nightmares that revealed more about the rapist's crimes than he should know. But the ugly truth was he could not get her out of his mind.

"If you're not careful, pal," he muttered, "you're going to find yourself obsessed with the woman."

Which would, he reminded himself yet again, be a major mistake.

He reached for the bottle of whiskey he'd switched back to after polishing off the brandy, then reminded himself of his resolution to cut down.

Even as he vowed to refrain from watching any more newscasts, or even think of her, the doorbell rang, resounding through the house like a death knell.

Roman felt a prickling sensation at the back of his neck. A second sense he'd always trusted kicked in, telling him that the object of all his consternation was standing on his front step.

"Yet another well-intentioned resolution goes down the tubes," he muttered. Surrendering to the inevitable, he went to answer the door.

8

THE ANGRY WORDS tumbling around in her mind were forgotten the moment the door swung open and Desiree found herself staring up into the most tortured, haggard face she'd ever seen.

She doubted he'd shaved since the night of the charity auction—the night he'd kissed her and stirred dark and dangerous feelings she'd been unable to put out of her mind.

The night he'd made her want him with a need that was almost as terrifying as it was unrelenting.

"You look like hell."

The bald, unflattering statement hit too close to home. Roman felt as if he'd been given a first-hand glimpse of hades lately. And the view was anything but comforting.

"Thanks for the compliment."

She refused to allow his acerbic tone to get under her skin. Something was very, very wrong here. And although she'd tried her best to tell herself that she didn't care about Roman Falconer, the truth was he'd touched something deep inside her. Even before that devastating kiss.

"You don't need compliments. What you need is a bath, a shave, a haircut and a decent meal. When was the last time you ate?"

He leaned one hand against the door frame, looming over her in a way designed to frighten her back to her television station. Where she belonged.

Where she'd be safe.

"Is that an offer to cook me dinner?"

"Obviously someone has to." She was as surprised as he by the words that had sprung uncensored from her lips. But now they were out, she refused to retract them. "Move out of the way, Falconer. And let me see if you've got anything besides ice cubes and soda water in your refrigerator."

"I drink my whiskey straight. Without ice." God help him—and her—he found himself stepping back, allowing her entry into his home. And, he feared, his life.

"Aren't you the macho one," she said with dry sarcasm. She glanced around, taking in the layer of dust that covered everything. It was even thicker than it had been four days ago. "You need a maid."

"I had a woman who came in once a week. She quit a couple of weeks ago."

"Scared her off, did you?" When she headed with uncanny instinct in the direction of the kitchen, Roman had no choice but to follow. "I'm not surprised."

"You don't seem to be running in the opposite direction."

"I don't scare that easily."

"I'm beginning to figure that out for myself."

"It's good to know that all that whiskey you've been drinking hasn't killed off all your brain cells," she retorted.

The kitchen looked every bit as bad as its owner.

"I take it back," Desiree said, eyeing the fast-food bags, foam containers and paper wrappings that littered the counters. "What I said about not scaring easily."

"I don't recall inviting you in."

Her chin flew up at his sarcastic tone. Her slender hands settled on her hips. "You bought a date with me, Falconer. And I'm damn well going to live up to my promise. Since you don't seemed inclined to go out, we're eating in. As soon as I shovel out some of this trash."

She took off her lightweight white wool coat, tossing it over the back of one of the kitchen chairs. She was dressed in the same clothes she'd worn on the earlier broadcast—a pink angora sweater that proved an attractive foil for her auburn hair, and a cream wool skirt that ended midthigh.

"I don't suppose you have an apron anywhere around this dump?"

"Sorry."

"I figured that was asking the impossible." She breathed a frustrated sigh. "If I ruin this sweater, you're buying me a new one."

"That sounds more than fair." He glanced around, viewed the kitchen through her eyes and decided that the lady definitely had guts. "Are you always this impulsive?"

"That depends. In my work I tend to be detail obsessive. As for my life—" she shrugged "—I prefer to go with the flow."

Reluctantly intrigued by the forceful, take-charge aura surrounding a female who looked as delicate as Irish crystal, Roman decided that there was something to be said for going with the flow. "Why don't I help?"

She turned and gave him a long, judicious perusal, from the top of his shaggy dark head down to his bare feet. "You can help by getting out of my way and going upstairs and taking a shower. And while you're at it, get rid of that stubble. It may have worked for Don Johnson, but the eighties are over, you can only watch *Miami Vice* on cable in the middle of the night and I prefer my dates clean shaven."

When his grizzled face felt as if it were about to crack, Roman realized that once again Desiree had managed to do the impossible. She'd made him smile.

"Anyone ever tell you that you can be a real bossy little thing?"

"All the time. Most recently just today, as a matter of fact." She tossed her head. "And for the record, I've always considered it a compliment."

Damn the man! Even though he looked like death warmed over, and although she'd never been one of those women drawn to darkly tormented men, just being in close proximity to Roman made her blood hum distractingly in her veins.

The faintest of smiles hovered at the corners of his mouth, making her wonder whether if she went up on her toes and kissed him—really kissed him—she could make that smile move to his deep, unfathomable eyes.

Roman watched the questions swirling in her eyes. And the unwilling desire. He lifted his hand to her face, skimming back her rich, tawny hair, cupping her jaw with his palm.

"I don't know if I have what you need."

His deep voice was soft and rough at the same time. His guard dropped momentarily, giving her a glimpse of an edgy, masculine hunger. And something else. Something that appeared to be genuine concern.

Roman Falconer confused her.

He frightened her. Just a little.

He also fascinated her.

Understanding that he was not talking about the state of his pantry, Desiree decided that now that she'd come this far, she may as well follow through on her impulsive behavior.

Putting her hands on his shoulders, she turned him around and pushed a palm against his back. "Go clean up, Falconer. While I see if I can keep the health department from declaring this place a toxic waste site."

Even as he told himself that he was a selfish son-of-a-bitch for not sticking to his plan to keep away from Desiree, Roman left the kitchen, heading upstairs to do as instructed.

Unsurprisingly, Roman's refrigerator was not exactly a treasure trove of culinary delights. A quick glance revealed a six pack of Dixie beer, a half-empty bottle of catsup, a quarter pound of butter with toast crumbs scattered across one end, some Dijon mustard and a wedge of moldy green cheese. Fortunately, she had better luck with the freezer.

While she whipped together some mustard and butter to top the lamb chops that, after thawing in the microwave, she stuck under the broiler, Desiree asked herself what on earth she was doing, cooking for a man she wasn't even sure she liked. A man whose haunted dark eyes reminded her of a Gothic hero. Heathcliffe, perhaps, who'd been doomed from the beginning to a life of torment and despair.

Oh, yes, there was too much about Roman Falconer that mirrored Emily Brontë's savagely dark character, she mused as she opened the bottle of merlot she'd discovered and poured herself a glass. And although Desiree liked to think of herself as a charitable person, she'd never considered herself much of a caretaker, let alone a savior of tortured souls.

Yet for some reason she could not comprehend, here she was, cleaning counters, cooking lamb chops and digging through cupboards searching for spices she could sprinkle on the pasta she'd decided to make as a side dish.

Thinking back on the other night, when he'd saved her from that cretin by paying an outrageously inflated price for a night on the town, Desiree reluctantly admitted Roman could be charming.

"But," she reminded herself under her breath as she stirred the pot of fettuccine bubbling away on the top of the stove, "that's what they say about the devil, too."

"Did someone call my name?" a deep voice asked from the doorway.

Turning around, Desiree realized all too well what she was doing here. Like it or not, although it made not a lick of sense, she was drawn to Roman in some mysterious way that was too powerful to resist.

His hair, which was still too long for conventional standards, gleamed like jet in the overhead light. His shaven face revealed a firm, square jaw. Experiencing a sudden, inexplicable need to touch that deep cleft in his chin, she tightened her fingers around the stem of her wineglass.

"You know what they say," she said with a casualness she was a very long way from feeling. She took what she hoped would be a calming sip of wine and eyed him over the rim of the glass. "Speak of the devil and you'll see the tip of his tail."

Her voice, schooled for television, remained smooth and steady. But the edgy emotion in her too-wide eyes gave her away.

"Is that really how you see me?" When he crossed the room to her, Desiree unconsciously took a few steps backward until she ran into the counter. "As a devil?"

She was quite literally trapped, the hard, cold ceramic tile against her back a striking contrast to the dis-

turbingly male body just inches away. A body that
radiated warmth and tightly controlled tension.

She stiffened as he reached out. Held her breath as his
fingers tightened in her hair.

"I don't know. Are you?" She'd tried for flippancy and
failed.

"I don't know."

He plucked the glass from her stiff fingers, turning it
until the faint pink smear of lipstick on the crystal rim
was facing him. With his dark, fathomless eyes on hers,
he lifted the glass and drank.

Watching that firmly cut mouth intimately embracing the same place her lips had touched was enough to
make Desiree tremble.

Roman, who never missed a thing, put the glass down
on the tile counter she'd recently scrubbed and began
running his hands down her arms in a way she found
anything but soothing.

"Are you cold?"

Far from it. She was burning up. From the inside out.
"No," she managed to murmur, her voice just decibels
above a whisper.

"Then you must be frightened."

He ran that treacherous hand down her arm again,
linking their fingers together as he had the other night on
the dance floor. When he brushed his lips across her
knuckles, Desiree felt herself going weak in the knees. No
man, she thought desperately, should possess this much
sexual power.

"I think I am," she admitted in that throaty voice that
had made her so popular among male viewers. A silky
voice that slipped beneath his skin, tantalized him in
ways that had him thinking of all the things he wanted
to do to her. With her.

"Of me?" He turned their joined hands and pressed a light kiss against the inside of her wrist, rewarded when he felt her pulse leap.

"No." Strangely, it was mostly the truth. The way he was looking at her, hard and deep, as if he could see all the way inside her to the passionate secrets lurking in her soul, kept Desiree from trying to get away with the convenient lie. "Well, perhaps just a little," she amended.

"That's probably wise." When he touched the tip of his tongue to the sensitive flesh his lips had warmed, Desiree drew in a quick, sharp breath.

"I suppose so." Perhaps he *was* the devil, she considered wildly, as fire flashed through her veins. "But most of all, I'm afraid of us."

"Us?"

The scent emanating from her skin was distracting Roman, making him forget that while standing under that streaming hot water in his shower, he'd sworn that he was going to come downstairs, thank her for her troubles and send the lady on her way.

"You." She lifted a hand to his shoulder, branding him through his shirt with her tender touch. "And me."

Unconsciously, she leaned toward him, her lips parting ever so slightly, her eyes gleaming with a gilt-edged, feminine invitation that Roman found nearly impossible to resist.

"Us together," she said softly.

Her lips were a silken lure, entrapping Roman in the grip of something as powerful as it was primal. He could have her. Here. Now. Before either of them had time to consider all the reasons why it would be wrong.

"Believe me, sweetheart, I know the feeling."

The air around them grew thick and heavy and sparked with electricity.

This is crazy, Roman told himself yet again. *Control.* It was imperative that he regain control. Not just of his body, but of this potentially perilous situation.

Even as he told himself that, as he gazed down into her exquisite face, Roman found himself wanting to drag her to the brick floor, strip her naked and bury himself inside her, to feel her hot and tight and wet around him.

This is insane, Desiree told herself through her swirling senses. Her mind, usually so organized and efficient, was reeling with images, all of them erotic, all of them having to do with Roman.

She imagined his mouth on her throat, her breast, could feel the scrape of teeth against her nipple. She envisioned his jet hair skimming across her breasts, his hot breath heating her flesh, trailing a fiery path down her body, until . . .

No! She shook her head in stunned disbelief and made a desperate attempt to deny the sexual desire that had risen, unbidden, like a fever in her blood.

Once again time seemed suspended as they each fought private, internal battles. A fist tightened in her stomach. Then lower. And although she'd always believed such a notion to be impossible, Desiree could feel herself going weak in the knees.

Roman lowered his head until his lips were a whisper away from hers, watching as her eyes drifted shut in anticipation of his kiss. It would be so easy. So wrong.

He paused, a desperate man caught on the edge of a jagged, treacherous cliff. One more step and they'd both go tumbling off into space. But perhaps the fatal fall would be worth it, he mused, tracing the shape of those ripe pink lips with the roughened pad of his thumb.

He reminded himself that he'd always been known for the ability to shut himself off from all emotions. He knew the nickname he'd earned during his years as a district attorney, and while some men might have found the description unflattering, Roman had always been vaguely proud of having earned it in the first place.

For five years he'd maintained an unprecedented conviction rate by keeping a cool head in the courtroom while prosecuting the perpetrators of the parish's most heinous crimes. And just as it had been vital back then, some cold-blooded logic was definitely in order right now.

At the last minute, a conscience he'd not been aware of possessing until recently, when the rapes had begun occurring, kicked in, and he managed to pull back. Both physically and emotionally.

"Are those lamb chops?"

"What?" Desiree blinked like a woman coming out of a trance. Her mind had been drifting in some floaty, warm place, prepared for the voluptuous pleasure she sensed he could bring to her. Instead, his casual, matter-of-fact statement brought her crashing back to earth.

What kind of man was Roman Falconer? she wondered, to be able to turn from hot to cold with one blink of those dangerous midnight eyes? She sagged against the counter, feeling as if she'd been put through an emotional wringer.

Roman viewed the disappointment in those lovely, liquid eyes and felt an answering regret deep inside him. "Are you broiling lamb chops?"

"Oh." She glanced around blankly at the stove, as if seeing it for the first time. "That was the plan."

Although he couldn't remember the last time he'd eaten, the aroma drifting from the oven, along with the clouds of steam rising from the boiling copper kettle, made Roman suddenly realize that he was famished. And not just for Desiree, although that hunger had not abated in the least.

"And a great plan it is, too." Unable to resist one last touch, he ran his palm down her hair, undeterred when she jerked away. "Thank you."

She was furious at him. Furious at him for toying with her emotions. Furious enough to want to cry. That had to be the reason she felt the hot sting of tears behind her eyelids, Desiree assured herself. She would not allow herself to care about a man who couldn't even care about himself.

It was one thing to lie to him about her unruly, confused feelings. That was, given the circumstances, only prudent behavior. The problem was she'd begun lying to herself as well.

The truth was that she *did* want him. Worse yet, she cared about him. Too much for comfort.

"I enjoy cooking." Her tone turned as casual as his. "Unfortunately, with my hours at the station, I don't have much time for it."

He could feel her distancing herself from the situation, from him, and realized it was for the best. "Well, whenever you find yourself feeling domestic," he suggested, turning away to pour a glass of wine for himself, "feel free to drop by."

"I'll keep that in mind." When hell froze over. If she actually managed to escape from here tonight with her heart intact, she wasn't ever coming back.

That was, she admitted, as she watched him lift his wineglass to those harsh, masculine lips, another lie. For someone who'd always had a very strong sense of where she was going, where she wanted to be, Desiree realized that somehow, when she wasn't looking, she'd lost control where Roman was concerned.

As he watched the unwilling emotion flood into her eyes, Roman took a long gulp of the merlot. It was, he decided, going to be a very long evening.

Somehow they managed to keep the conversation going over dinner. By mutual, unspoken consent, they did not discuss the French Quarter rapes. Instead they shared selected bits of biography.

Although they'd both grown up in the exclusive environs of Audubon Place, they'd never met, due to Roman being six years older and Desiree having spent most of her youthful years in boarding schools in New York, Arizona and Switzerland.

"I met your grandmother once," Roman revealed. "At one of my parent's dinner parties." He frowned as he thought back on that evening, wondering how such a grim-faced harridan could possibly be related to this warm, emotional woman. "She was a rather formidable woman."

"Yes." Desiree's fingers tightened around her fork. "She was that."

She'd also been as cold as a glacier and as unfeeling as a stone. Desiree had been ten years old when her parents had died and she'd been sent to live with Olivia Porter, her maternal grandmother. By the time she was eleven, she understood all too well why her mother had run away from home at the age of seventeen to marry Lucien—Lucky—Dupree. A fisherman from Iberville, Lucky was nothing like the wealthy young men of privilege and rank Katherine Porter had been accustomed to.

But he'd laughed easily and often and had loved his wife with a warmth and passion she'd never known. When, nine months after their elopement, Desiree was born, he'd loved his daughter, too. The only cloud in their life was that Katherine could not have any more children, but since Lucky had a large extended family, that hadn't seemed a tragedy.

And then Katherine Porter Dupree, who'd never had so much as a cold, became ill. Unwilling to spend money on a doctor, she'd shrugged off the pain and lethargy until it was too late. Six months before Desiree's tenth birthday, her mother had died of ovarian cancer. The funeral was held in Iberville, paid for with donations from Lucky's friends and family. Olivia Porter, notified of her only daughter's death, did not attend.

Two weeks after her mother's ashes were laid to rest in the Dupree family tomb, tragedy had struck again. Lucky was on the way home from delivering nutria pelts to a buyer in Baton Rouge when the steering went out on his ancient rattletrap of a truck, sending it plummeting into the bayou. In an attempt to comfort Desiree, friends assured her that her daddy was now with her mommy.

Which didn't provide all that much solace, since she'd been left behind. Lucky's sister Evangeline had immediately taken Desiree in, treating her like one of her own children.

Which was when Olivia had finally chosen to put in an appearance. She'd arrived at the remote, ramshackle bayou home, court papers in hand, declaring herself custodian of her only grandchild. And although Evangeline, backed up by her husband and all eight children, had protested hotly, Olivia Porter's considerable political clout had prevailed.

But not before subjecting Desiree to a custody fight that had made all the papers, caused her uncle Jean Luc's fishing boat—which he'd heavily mortgaged to pay legal costs—to be repossessed by the bank and put a ten-year-old girl in the center ring of a public three-ring circus.

Roman watched the emotions, none of them pleasant, move across Desiree's face as she related the story. "It must have been difficult," he said. "Losing your parents at such a tender age."

His words jerked her back to the presence. "It wasn't what I would have chosen." Her tone revealed not a scintilla of emotion. Her angora-clad shoulders lifted in an uncaring shrug.

But Roman, who was watching her carefully, did not miss the cloud that moved across her eyes. "I was adopted," he said, feeling the need to share some equally intimate piece of his past.

"Really?" She remembered her grandmother talking about the Falconers—Olivia Porter had disapproved of Mrs. Falconer working outside the home, Desiree recalled—and wondered why that little tidbit had not come up. "I didn't know that."

"Not many people do."

He ran his hand around the rim of the glass and remembered all too well the day he'd learned the truth himself. He'd been twelve years old. And after he'd listened to his parents' carefully chosen words, he'd gone on a rock-throwing spree, breaking windows in houses up and down the private, gated street. One of those homes, he recalled now, had belonged to Olivia Porter.

"I didn't take it at all well, at first," he admitted.

At least she'd lost her parents to death. Desiree wondered how it must feel to have been abandoned by your natural parents. "And later?"

He remembered his mom and dad showing up at the police station. Remembered the licking he'd gotten from his father when he returned home. Remembered how they'd all cried afterward.

Remembered also how it had taken six months of paper-route money to pay his father back for replacing all those windows.

"It finally sunk in that whatever the circumstances of my birth, I was damn lucky to have landed in a home with parents who loved me. And wanted me."

The part of Desiree that had spent so many years of her childhood longing for a home envied Roman. The reporter in her was curious about how he'd felt, knowing he was adopted.

"Were you ever tempted to try to find your natural parents?"

"Of course." Roman found it a little ironic that they were having their first fairly normal conversation over something that once, albeit years ago, had caused him so much pain. "My parents assured me that when I was eighteen, they'd do everything they could to help me."

"And did they?"

"No. Because by the time I was eighteen I was long past caring. I was smart enough by then to realize that whatever the circumstances of my birth, my real parents were the couple who had volunteered to be around to hold my head when I was throwing up with the flu, to play catch in the backyard, to clean up after the puppy I wanted so badly when I was eight and to provide that day-to-day support and stability kids need."

He held up his hand, displaying a ring fashioned of antique gold with a onyx stone in the center. "This belonged to my grandfather. My father gave it to me after he brought me home from the police station. To underscore the point that I was a Falconer."

"You were lucky."

He smiled at that, the first genuine, uncensored smile she'd witnessed. "Yes." Amazingly, the shared revelation seemed to banish the strain that had been hovering over the kitchen. And although the sexual tension that had sparked between them so quickly and so often had not diminished, both Roman and Desiree found themselves able to put it aside, for now.

The conversation flowed smoothly, moving from a discussion of her work at WSLU to social gossip about people they both knew to his previous career as district attorney.

"Did you enjoy working as a prosecutor?"

"I enjoyed putting the bad guys away."

"From what I've heard and read, you were obviously very good at your job. But then you left." She eyed him curiously over the rim of her wineglass. "Why?"

"The reason wasn't exactly earth-shattering. I always wanted to write, and I suppose the stories I came up with were a natural outgrowth from my work."

"Writing crime novels isn't that unusual for a former cop or prosecutor," she agreed.

"True." He nodded. "At the time, I was accused of being burned out from dealing with man's inhumanity to man on an everyday basis." A column about him had run in the *Times Picayune* the day after he'd announced that he was retiring. Roman had found the rationale in the piece ridiculously simplistic. "Actually, it was more the frustration of having reality not live up to the fantasy I held. I didn't want to accept the fact that I couldn't win them all. And of course, when I did get a conviction, it was often too late for the victim."

"Ah." Desiree thought she understood. "You had a Superman complex." In that one way he reminded her a lot of O'Malley.

"I don't know about that." He shrugged, looking vaguely embarrassed. "I do know that when I'm writing a book, I control the world I've created. And the characters in it. Nothing happens without my consent."

That was not precisely true—not any longer. But Roman was damned if he was going to share that lethal little piece of information with her. "And when the book's finished, the good guys have won." *Lord, he hoped so.*

"I've always liked happy endings," she agreed with a smile, even as she wondered at the reason for that shadow that had drifted across his eyes again.

Shaking off the renewed gloom, Roman launched into a wicked description of a recent book tour he'd recently completed—"a trip to hell and back in fourteen days"— that had Desiree in stitches. One of his more outrageous stories, regarding a reader who stood up in the Oprah audience and swore he was her long-lost husband, broke her up completely.

"I think I know her husband," she said at last, wiping tears of laughter from her eyes. "I was married to him in a past life."

"You believe in past lives?"

"No." Her grin was quick and bright and lit up her eyes in a way that made them gleam like a pair of antique gold coins. "But *he* does."

"Ah." He nodded and refilled their glasses with the last of the merlot. "Another secret admirer. Perhaps he's the one who sent the flowers."

"Perhaps." She felt a sudden chill she knew had nothing to do with the December night. Enjoying herself too much to dwell on the rapist who had yet to contact her again, she shook it off.

He caught the faint change in her mood and wondered at its cause. A vision flashed at the front of his mind—a vision of Desiree, standing beside a small pond. She was wearing a filmy white nightgown that was being blown against her by an icy wind. Her hair was loose and free, tumbling around her bare shoulders like flames. She was clutching a bouquet of bloodred roses to her breast.

When he viewed the tears shimmering in her wide eyes and trailing down her cheeks in long silver ribbons, Roman felt as if someone had suddenly stuck a stiletto into his heart.

"Roman?" She watched as he closed his eyes. His mouth was twisted in a grimace of something that looked a great deal like pain. "Are you all right?"

Perhaps he'd looked so dreadful when she'd first shown up because he was ill. She was considering asking if she should call a doctor when he dragged his hand down his face and finally answered her.

"Yes." The single word was muffled by his palm. "Sorry. I was thinking about something."

"Your book?" He'd alluded to a new book he was working on, but hadn't told her anything about the plot.

"Yeah." It was true, as far as it went. Roman wondered what she'd say if he told her that somehow his rebellious muse had altered certain physical and behavioral characteristics regarding his heroine until she bore a striking similarity to Desiree.

"I'm sorry." He shook off the disturbing feeling and tried to remind himself that only moments before he'd actually been enjoying himself. "It's just that sometimes, when I'm deep in a book, my mind suddenly drifts back to it."

"I can understand that." Deciding that her imagination was playing tricks on her again, she opted to put the problem aside. For now. "Is the book you're working on going to be set in New Orleans?" The other four that she'd read had all been located in and around the city.

"Mostly. Along with quite a few scenes in bayou country."

That had been another surprise. As was his habit, honed during years of law school, then of working as a prosecutor, Roman planned out his plots in exacting detail. In his previous books, he hadn't deviated from the synopsis. This time not only had his heroine recently taken on the characteristics of Desiree Dupree, but another character had risen full-blown from the murky depths of his imagination. A dark, destructive devil born in the mysterious mists of Louisiana's bayou.

Desiree shivered at the involuntary image created by his answer. "I can tell this is going to be another book I'm going to have to read with all the lights on."

He shrugged. "As my agent always says, sex and violence sells." He provided violence. In spades. While Desiree handled sex.

"That's what they say," she agreed. His eyes had narrowed in an expression she couldn't interpret, but which left her feeling uncomfortable nevertheless.

A silence stretched between them as Roman waited for her to reveal her secret writing success and Desiree wondered yet again if he knew she was the author of those books of erotica she'd found in his library. No, she assured herself. She'd hidden her tracks too well.

"My villain this time is a rapist," he volunteered.

Considering the fact that a serial rapist was currently running loose in the Quarter, Desiree found the coincidence less than comforting.

"Your last book had a rapist for a villain," she responded. "If you're not careful, Roman, you're going to get in a rut."

"The guy from *Killing Her Softly* escapes."

"Peter Harrington escapes? From prison?"

"From the infirmary. It's a very clever getaway."

"Why?"

"Why does he escape? For the same reason anyone else goes over the wall. He doesn't like being locked up."

"No, that's not what I meant." She sent him a cool, speculative look that was mostly feigned. "Why are you writing about him again?" The man was one of the most evil fictional characters she'd ever encountered. The thought that anyone like him might be running loose in real life was more than a little discomfiting.

"The truth?" he asked. How could he explain that he had no choice? That he was driven to witness his villainous character's latest rash of increasingly brutal crimes? Crimes that, as impossible as it seemed, were turning out to be all too real.

She nodded.

"I don't know."

His reply was only three little words. But although it made not a lick of sense, Desiree detected a hidden meaning beneath them. Another silence settled in the room, lingering until she didn't know whether to scream or to cry. She was just about to do both when a sudden sound shattered the suspended mood.

"Saved by the beeper," Roman drawled with heavy irony as she practically leapt from the table and retrieved the black device from her purse.

"It's one of my producers. Adrian Beauvier."

"Does he usually call you—" Roman glanced up at the clock "—this late?"

"He's like the Café du Monde. Open all night," she answered. "May I use your phone?"

"Of course." He realized that any plans he might have had for taking advantage of their newly established congeniality would have to be postponed.

"Hi, it's me," she said when the voice on the other end answered.

"It's him again." The producer did not need to elaborate. Desiree began rubbing her arm with her free hand, to ward off the sudden chill. "They found the girl in Whooping Crane Pond at Audubon park."

"*In* the pond?" she asked with surprise, drawing a sharp glance from Roman.

"I mean *in* the pond. The cops are being real coy on the radio, but it looks as if our rapist has upped the ante. He killed this one, Des."

It was what she'd been dreading. As she hung up the phone, Desiree decided that she could no longer honor the deal she'd made with O'Malley.

If the city council didn't care enough to protect the innocent women of New Orleans from this monster, then she was going to have to warn them of the dangers.

And if it took reaching out to the rapist-turned-killer, offering him a chance for the publicity he'd been seeking, well, she'd do that, too.

9

THE SCENE WAS much the same as it had been at the cemetery.

Lights lit up the park like daylight. There were numerous patrol cars along with an ambulance. Yellow police tape marked the boundary.

Desiree, who'd learned to observe such things, noticed that there were also differences. Unlike the other night, the driver this time was standing beside his red-and-white ambulance, smoking a cigarette, which suggested that his services were not going to be immediately needed.

Also, most of the uniformed officers had been kept on the civilian side of the yellow tape, the better, Desiree knew, to protect the crime scene.

Adrian was right. With this strike, the French Quarter rapist had obviously upped the ante.

O'Malley, unsurprisingly, had responded accordingly.

"I'm sorry, Ms. Dupree." One of the officers, whom she recognized as a rookie patrol cop in the Garden District where the park was located, stopped her as she tried to duck under the tape. "But I'm not supposed to let anyone past. Detective O'Malley's orders."

She felt the familiar surge of frustration, considered arguing the standard line about freedom of the press, then almost immediately decided that Michael was right on this one. As much as she wanted access, she wanted this monster stopped even more.

"I understand." She did, perfectly. But that didn't mean she had to like it. There was also no way she was going to leave without a story. She turned the possibilities around in her mind and decided nothing ventured, nothing gained.

"Could you please do me one little favor, Officer?"

Her voice lowered in that silky, soothing tone that had served her well during her tenure at the station. It was her I-want-to-be-your-friend voice. A voice that assured and calmed even as it encouraged compliance; a voice designed to help her get her way in sticky, difficult situations. It was also, undeniably, the voice of a woman coaxing a man into doing what she wanted him to.

There had been times, in the beginning, when Desiree experienced a bit of guilt for using her feminine wiles to get a story. She'd finally decided that if any man was chauvinistic enough to drop his guard simply because she was a woman, he deserved what he got.

As it had in the past, the smoky tone began to work now. She watched the slight softening of the young man's jaw, saw the faintest relaxation in his guard-position stance.

"If I can, Ms. Dupree." The qualification reassured her. She wouldn't want to think any one of New Orleans's finest was a pushover for a pretty face and a dulcet voice.

"Could you please ask Detective O'Malley if, when he can spare a moment, I could speak with him?"

The cop glanced over his shoulder at the bustling crime scene, then back at Desiree. Then his attention was drawn to a new arrival.

Desiree turned as well, viewed the man climbing out of an unmarked black sedan and realized that the fact that the medical examiner had arrived so soon proved yet again how seriously everyone was taking this latest escalation.

"I was ordered to stay here," the rookie said as he lifted the tape to allow the M.E. to pass. "To guard the perimeter."

"But surely it would only take a moment." She refrained, just barely, from putting her hand on his arm. "I promise not to move from this spot."

"I don't know. . . ." He was looking decidedly torn. "Even if I were to ask, I can't guarantee Detective O'Malley will be able to speak with you anytime soon."

"Things look serious," she observed, trying a different tack.

"Crime is always serious. Ma'am," he added, making her feel, although she was only twenty-five herself, about as old as dirt.

Then again, she figured she'd probably seen a lot more crime than this fresh-faced rookie had. "Of course it is." Her expression was appropriately grave. But as badly as she felt for the victim, she had a job to do.

As she began to work the cop, Desiree got caught up in her interview enough that the initial chill she'd felt upon hearing the news, began to warm. There was nothing like a major story to start her blood pumping. "But, of course, there *are* varying levels of crime," she suggested. "Which is why it's such a tragedy that this time the rapist has murdered his victim."

As he watched the ambulance attendants wheel the gurney over to the pond, the distracted patrolman murmured a vague agreement.

Bingo. She now had her confirmation. Her mind surged into high gear, already writing her lead-in. "So he did kill her." She managed, just barely, to keep from sounding triumphant.

Belatedly realizing that he'd been expertly baited, the young cop twisted his head back to Desiree and shot her a chagrined, irritated look. "I'll go give Detective O'Malley your message," he muttered after a brief pause. Being outwitted by a woman was bad enough. Being manipulated into leaking information on a capital case by a reporter was enough to make any cop—rookie or grizzled veteran—angry.

Desiree smiled sweetly. Agreeably. Having achieved her goal, she could afford to be generous. "Thank you, Officer."

"You should be ashamed of yourself," a low rumbling voice observed.

Desiree grinned up at Sugar, who had materialized beside her during her conversation with the patrolman. "Who, me?"

He shook his head at her display of feigned innocence. "Taking advantage of a poor green-as-grass boy that way."

"That poor green boy just happens to be a New Orleans policeman," she stated. "Which means he may as well learn to keep his mouth shut now, rather than spilling the beans in the future to some unscrupulous reporter who doesn't realize there's a very fine line between freedom of the press and the need for police to withhold certain information in order to solve their crime, thus protecting society."

"You learn those pretty words outta some journalism textbook you read in college? At Hahvaard?" He added a Boston twang to the word.

"Actually, I picked them up last year. From the gospel of Detective Michael Patrick O'Malley."

"That sound like the man," he agreed with a nod of his enormous bald, black head. "It also sounds as if you're indulging in a bit of self-justification."

Her eyes narrowed as she looked a long way up at him. It was not the first time she'd witnessed Sugar's instantaneous transition from black street rapper to someone who sounded as if he possessed a degree in psychology or philosophy. The enigmatic man was definitely not what he appeared at first glance, she decided, thinking of O'Malley's description of being layered like an onion.

That thought brought up another that was never far from her mind these days. Roman Falconer.

From the first moment she'd seen the former district attorney, she'd been drawn to him in ways she could not begin to understand. And although she considered herself a rational sort of person, whenever she was around him, she found herself reacting with pure emotion.

Which was, of course, foolhardy with any man. But even more deadly with a man like Roman.

That thought led directly to yet another—a recent memory, only minutes old, of when her beeper had providentially sounded, rescuing her from a dangerously intimate moment. There was something that bothered her about that prolonged interlude. Something niggling at the far reaches of her mind; something she couldn't quite get a handle on.

Before she could figure out what it was, O'Malley began striding toward her, his expression as furious as she'd ever seen it. Beside her, Sugar lifted the portable videocam to his shoulder and began shooting.

"Good idea," Desiree murmured as she viewed the icy murder in the detective's eyes. "This way, if he kills me, you'll have the evidence on tape."

"'Less he kill me, too," Sugar suggested. "And from the look of him, that be a definitely possibility." He'd switched back into the street accent that added to his mystique.

"Well, if it isn't the Bobbsey Twins," O'Malley muttered scathingly. His sharp glare could have cut diamonds. "Don't you two have anything better to do with your nights than hang around crime scenes?"

"We're just doing our job, Detective." Desiree refused to let him annoy her.

"Since when does your job include harassing my men?"

She gave him her most-innocent look. "I was only asking him a few questions."

"His assignment was to keep civilians away from my crime scene. You got questions, ask me."

"Fine. I will." There was no point in telling him that she'd tried to do exactly that in the beginning and had only switched to pumping the patrolman when her game plan had begun to fall apart.

Desiree glanced over his shoulder to where the uniformed rookie was throwing up beneath an oak tree. "She must have been in the pond awhile."

Although she'd guess that it was the young cop's first close-up-and-personal look at a corpse, she suspected his reaction was due more to its condition.

Working in an area surrounded by water, Desiree had seen floaters before. Including one politician who, it was belatedly discovered, had won reelection with a few too many cemetery votes. Even for this state, where politics tended to be absolutely Byzantine, *that* was stepping over the line. When forced to resign, the depressed state senator had ended up taking a dive off the bridge into the river.

She'd been on the scene when he'd been fished out a week later. It was not a pretty sight.

"Best guess is a few days," O'Malley concurred. "A couple of kids making out in the gazebo spotted her."

Desiree glanced at the gazebo where she and O'Malley had sat in the warm December sun, drinking their coffee and arguing. "My God, Michael, she could have been there." When she began to shake from the inside out, she dug her teeth into her lower lip to steady herself. "Right below us."

"I've already thought of that." His eyes appeared haunted, revealing just how much this investigation was getting to him. "We'll know more after the M.E. is through with his autopsy."

Desiree watched the gurney with the black body bag being wheeled toward the waiting ambulance and empathized with the rookie. She suddenly felt more than a little sick herself. "I realize it's probably too early to tell, but—"

"It's the same guy," he finished for her.

She'd known it was. But somehow, hearing it made it seem so much more real. And threatening.

"The ribbons?" she asked, her voice a faint thread of sound.

"Yeah." His mouth was a harsh, tight line. "The bastard tied her up, undoubtedly raped her, then cut her throat. From ear to ear."

The familiar words echoed in Desiree's mind. It wasn't that unusual a way to kill someone. The fact that the slaves allegedly murdered at Roman's house had *also* been reported to have had their throats slashed was only a coincidence.

One more coincidence in a very long line of them. Beginning with Roman just happening by the cemetery the night the last girl had been raped. And then, of course, there was the little matter of Desiree having found her books in the man's personal library.

Which didn't mean a thing, she assured herself. Thousands of people owned copies of her novels. There were probably hundreds right here in New Orleans Parish alone.

When she became aware of both Sugar and O'Malley looking at her with curiosity, she realized she'd allowed her discomfort regarding Roman Falconer to show. "I don't suppose you have a name yet." This time her voice was brisk and professional.

"Not yet."

"But she's a prostitute?"

"Either that or Santa is missing an elf," he growled. "She was wearing one of those Santa's helper's outfits," he elaborated.

"She could be from one of the malls." Only yesterday Desiree had seen a similarly dressed young girl handing out candy canes at Jackson's Brewery.

"I suppose that's a possibility," he replied. "But how many of those girls have you seen wearing a red, fake-fur-trimmed garter belt?"

"Good point." She envisioned the girl as she must have looked when she'd made the fatal mistake of getting into a car with the wrong man. "You know," she mused out loud, "an outfit like that would be bound to draw attention. Even in the Quarter."

"The wrong kind of attention, as it turns out."

"True. But someone must have noticed her being picked up."

Although the street prostitutes were known for their colorful and often outrageous attire, Desiree guessed that anyone who'd wear an elf costume would be young. The victim had undoubtedly been another runaway. Once again Desiree thought back on how many times she'd wanted to run away herself during those painful teenage years when she'd been boarded out like some inconvenient pet her grandmother hadn't wanted to deal with.

Once again she thought about how desperately she'd yearned for love. Was that what those girls had been seeking? Had they also been looking for someone to hold them in the long, lonely hours of the night? Someone to make them feel appreciated? Valued? Loved?

It could have been her, she realized, her attention drawn to the ambulance that was pulling away with a lack of lights and sirens. If she hadn't had the warm memories of those early years with her parents to hang on to during the bleak times, she could have ended up as lost and drifting as the rapist's unfortunate victims.

"We're already running a check of the neighborhoods," O'Malley said. "There's nothing for you to do here, Desiree. Why don't you go home? I'll be holding a press conference at nine at the station. You can get your facts then."

"With the others." She frowned, putting away hurtful memories along with thoughts of those raped and murdered slaves allegedly buried in Roman's garden. "You promised me an exclusive, O'Malley."

"And you'll get one. When and if the creep ever calls you."

"What if he doesn't? What if he's already given up on me? Come on, Detective, surely I should get some little reward for having kept the story off the air."

"You'll be the first I call when we nab the guy."

"Thank you." She nodded, satisfied for the time being, at least.

"But for now, it's obvious that I can't keep this under wraps any longer. I've got to go public, Desiree. And that means a press conference."

It was exactly what she'd been lobbying for from the beginning. Still, she couldn't help wondering how such a decision would be viewed at the mayor's office. "This isn't going to make you real popular downtown," she said, telling him nothing he didn't already know.

"Tough." His expression was one she'd seen before—when he'd promised her that he'd nab her stalker. "I've got wide shoulders. I can handle a little political flack."

Ignoring Sugar's still-whirring videocam, Desiree put aside professionalism and lifted her hands to those wide shoulders. Going up on her toes, she kissed O'Malley's cheek. "It's times like this when I remember why I fell in love with you."

His large hands instinctively settled on her waist as the two of them exchanged a look rife with memories and regret. And, she thought, resignation. Although neither of them could possibly be called a quitter, their relationship simply would not have worked. No matter how hard they tried.

"You're right," she said when the moment drew out a bit longer than was comfortable. "I'd better go. And let you get back to work."

"I suppose you going home to bed would be too much to hope for?"

"I'll go home eventually. But first I've got to run by the station. Hey, as tragic as this is, it's still a scoop," she said quickly when she sensed he was prepared to argue. "Now that you've decided to go public, I've got to run with my story. Such as it is at this point."

He gave her one last long look. "Just be careful. I don't want to be pulling you from some damn duck pond."

"Never happen."

"You're not Wonder Woman," he reminded her.

"Believe me, O'Malley, I've already figured that out for myself."

She placed a call to Karyn from the cellular phone in her car. By the time she arrived at the station, the producer had arrived. The rest of the early morning crew showed up within minutes, and after a frenzied few hours writing copy and editing Sugar's video, Desiree repaired her makeup, brushed her hair and taped her report.

The first part was professional and to the point. The second part was a personal request to the rapist that she knew was going to make Detective First Class Michael O'Malley go absolutely ballistic.

"Wow!" Karyn leaned against the anchor desk and eyed Desiree with a mixture of admiration and worry. "That was quite a piece."

"Thank you." Suddenly emotionally and physically drained, Desiree gathered up her papers. It had been the right thing to do, she assured herself. The only thing she could do.

"You realize, of course, that you're a shoe-in for *Nightline* now."

"I wasn't thinking about *Nightline*," Desiree said. "I was thinking about all those potential victims." She dragged her hand through her hair in a weary gesture. "He has to be stopped."

"Not that I don't think you were brilliant, because you were, but I feel obliged to point out that stopping the guy is O'Malley's job."

"I realize that." Desiree stood up. "But even the Lone Ranger needed Tonto's help from time to time."

"You know, of course, that Michael isn't going to be at all happy when he sees this morning's broadcast," Karyn warned.

"He'll undoubtedly want to kill me," Desiree agreed. "I guess I'm just going to have to depend on you to use all your feminine wiles to keep that from happening."

When her comment caused a decidedly feminine blush, Desiree laughed. Then she left the station and drove through the dark and mostly deserted streets.

The first thing she saw as she pulled into the driveway of her Irish Channel Victorian cottage was the sleek black Porsche parked at the curb. When the driver's door opened, she immediately reached for her car phone, prepared to call 911. As the spreading glow of the street-light illuminated Roman's face, she breathed a sigh of relief.

"What are you doing here?" she demanded as she climbed out of her own car. She was irritated by the way just seeing the man could cause such an unwilling surge of pleasure.

He was moving toward her with his loose-hipped, predator's stride, but for some reason, this morning she didn't feel threatened. "I was worried about you," he said simply as they met halfway.

"I was working."

"Anyone ever tell you that you work too hard?"

All the time, she could have answered. "My work hours aren't any of your business," she said instead.

"That's what I kept telling myself these past hours while I've been parked outside your house waiting for you to come home. And you know what?"

"What?"

"I couldn't make myself believe it."

Desiree shook her head. "I really don't want this," she murmured. She had too much on her plate right now to handle any new relationships. Let alone one that was already proving intensely complex.

She was visibly exhausted, Roman noted. Her always fair complexion was unnaturally pale, giving her face the look of fragile bone china. "Want me to leave?"

The funny thing was, she didn't. Telling herself that it was only because she was still too wired from taping that news segment to get any sleep, she said, "Now that you're here, you may as well come in."

He'd certainly received warmer invitations in his day. But, willing to take Desiree any way he could get her, Roman followed her into the house.

10

THE INTERIOR OF Desiree's house proved to be as feminine as her name.

It was obvious to Roman that here, in the privacy of her home, she allowed her emotions free reign. Violets bloomed on the cream, papered walls, needlepoint carpets were scattered about the stenciled, pine-plank floors. Lacy white curtains topped with billowy balloon valences framed the Gothic arched windows.

Although the cottage was small, the high ceilings and airy furniture gave it a feeling of spaciousness.

"You've put in a lot of hard work," Roman said.

As she shrugged out of her coat, Desiree glanced around as if seeing the living room for the very first time. The house, located in a working-class district of the city that was undergoing regentrification, had fallen into disrepair when she'd discovered it.

Although the poor little Victorian cottage had appeared on its last legs, the structure proved sound, and fortunately, some distant owner in the 1950s had upgraded the plumbing and electrical systems.

Which, other than the new roof that was needed to stop the streaks left on layers of peeling wallpaper every time it rained, left Desiree with mostly a great deal of cosmetic work.

"It's been a labor of love," she admitted, more than a little pleased with the results. She hung the coat on an ornate brass coatrack she'd discovered in an antique store across the street from the station.

"It shows."

He paused in front of a gilt mirror that had been hung on the flowered wall with a lavender satin ribbon. Her exquisite face was reflected in the glass, and Roman decided that if she ever looked at him with the warmth of emotion that was glowing in her eyes right now as she studied the results of her renovations, he'd marry her on the spot. Because even with her pallor and those smudged shadows beneath her eyes, she was the loveliest woman he'd ever seen. He slipped his hands into the back pockets of his jeans to keep from touching her.

"So," he said with forced casualness as he turned back toward her, "what was important enough to call you out in the middle of the night?"

The warmth immediately left those gilt eyes, like a candle snuffed out by a Gulf Coast hurricane. "It was the rapist."

Something went very, very still inside Roman. Needing something—anything—to do, he reached out and straightened a picture. The framed snapshot was of a young girl with wild, windblown hair the color of flame. She was wearing an oversized T-shirt, a pair of too-large jeans rolled up to the knees, and she was carrying a bamboo fishing rod. The grin on her freckled face revealed immense pride in her catch. Along with a missing front tooth.

"He struck again?" Roman was amazed that his voice sounded so matter-of-fact.

"They found the girl in Whooping Crane Pond."

An image sprung full-blown into his mind, like a wartime flashback: the vision he'd had during dinner, of Desiree dressed in a filmy white nightgown, standing beside a small pond, a bouquet of bloodred roses clutched to her breast.

"This time he killed her," Desiree revealed.

Horrifyingly, Roman already knew that. Unconsciously, he glanced down at his hands, half expecting to see them covered in some young girl's blood.

He wanted to ask more questions. But viewing Desiree's obvious exhaustion, he decided that whatever answers she could provide would have to wait.

"Look," he suggested, "I'm just keeping you up. I'd better go."

"No," she said quickly. She wasn't eager to be alone. Not after what had happened. "Don't leave." Under normal conditions she never would have stooped to something that sounded uncomfortably like begging. But these were far-from-normal conditions. "I'm too wound up to get any sleep. And to tell you the truth, I'd like company."

From the embarrassment in her eyes, Roman suspected Desiree was not accustomed to asking for favors from anyone. Which was why, although he knew that to remain would be to sink deeper into the quicksand his life seemed to be immersed in these days, he found it impossible to refuse her softly spoken request.

"Why don't I make you some tea?" he suggested.

She answered with a faint, reminiscent smile. "That's the second time you've offered me tea."

"Blame it on my mother. Being half-English, she's always believed tea to be the universal antidote to most of life's problems."

"I envy your mother her belief system." She also envied Roman his mother.

Suddenly more tired than she'd ever been in her life, she sank down onto the flower-sprigged cushion of the white wicker sofa and kicked off the Italian pumps she'd been wearing for nearly the past twenty-four hours.

"What can it hurt?" She dragged a weary hand through her hair. "I'll try the tea." Her hand dropped to her side. "The kitchen's in there." Her words had begun to slur. Too worn out to point, she nodded toward an arched doorway.

"I can manage. Although I'm admittedly not the most domestic guy on the planet, I *am* capable of boiling water."

For not the first time, Roman realized how delicate she was. Her mother, after all, had been a Porter. But her father had been a Louisiana Cajun who'd known how to live life to its fullest. A man accustomed to going with the flow. The very fact that Katherine Porter had dared to risk her own mother's wrath and elope with Lucky Dupree, turning her back on wealth and privilege for love, proved she, too, had possessed a passionate nature. And both these individuals' blood was flowing through Desiree's veins.

The thought of her bringing all that passion to their lovemaking—which Roman had already decided was inevitable—made him want to scoop her up from that feminine couch and carry her into the bedroom which he suspected would be every bit as romantic as the living room.

Because he wanted her to be a willing participant, he resisted and went into the kitchen to prepare the tea he suspected neither of them really wanted. As he left the room, Desiree leaned her head against the back cushion, allowed her eyes to drift shut and promptly fell asleep.

Roman found her right where he'd left her, looking deathly pale and vulnerable. The sight pulled unbidden, unwanted, heretofore unexperienced emotional chords deep inside him, leading him to curse softly under his breath.

He put the cups onto a glass-topped wicker table. Then he bent down and picked up her stocking-clad feet, swiveling her legs until she was lying down. She didn't move a muscle. Not even when he lifted her head to put the fringed pillow beneath it. Not when he covered her with the lacy white, Irish wool blanket he took from the back of a neighboring chair.

Her hair spilled over the velvet pillow like molten bronze. Her lashes were dark and spiky against her cheeks, and her rosy lips were slightly parted in a way that made him think of Sleeping Beauty awaiting the kiss of her prince to awaken her. The problem with that little scenario, he decided, was that Desiree might be a beauty. But he was no prince.

Which wasn't quite accurate, he amended, thinking back on the nickname his fellow prosecutors had given him during his days as district attorney.

Not wanting to wake her up, but not wanting to leave her, either, Roman sat down in a chair across from the couch. As he drank the Chinese tea and watched Desiree sleep, he found himself wondering about the odds of the Dark Prince ever winning the fair maiden.

POUNDING ON HER DOOR awakened Desiree from her dreamless, exhausted sleep.

"Dammit, Desiree," the deep voice shouted from the other side of the door. "I know you're in there. So open up!"

She sighed and dragged a hand through her uncombed hair. "Hold your horses, I'm coming." She forced herself off the couch and opened the door. "Can I help you, Officer?"

"I ought to beat you," O'Malley growled as he marched past her into the house.

"Then I'd have to report you for police brutality." She shut the door and followed him into the living room.

"Since the thought of applying a few lashes with a rubber hose against that tight backside is seeming more and more appealing with each passing day, I'm willing to risk it. What the hell did you think you were doing?"

She folded her arms across her chest. "I assume you're referring to my morning report."

"Where you invite the creep to rape you, too."

"I don't believe that's what I was suggesting."

"You offered to talk with the guy, dammit! 'Anytime. Anywhere,'" he quoted.

"I was inviting him to turn himself in to authorities. I merely suggested I'd be willing to accompany him to the police station, to ensure his safety."

"Since when are you so freaking worried about a murderer's safety?"

"I'm worried about all the other potential victims."

Needing coffee, she turned and walked into the adjoining kitchen. When she saw the cold tea in a cup on the counter, she remembered asking Roman to make her some. Great company she'd been, falling asleep on him after asking him to stay with her. She turned and saw an empty tea cup on the coffee table, and she flushed, wondering just how long he'd sat there in the wing chair, watching her sleep, before he'd tired of the vigil and gone home.

Pushing Roman out of her mind, she concentrated on O'Malley and the matter at hand. "I thought the rapist

might be worried about suffering an 'accidental' injury
if he turned himself in. So I offered to go with him."

"You had no right interfering in my case."

"I wasn't interfering."

"The hell you weren't!" His hands were curled into fists
at his side. From the way he was flexing his fingers, Desiree had the feeling he was anxious to hit something.
"You finally gave the sicko creep the publicity he's been
seeking. What makes you think he won't rape again, just
to get more television coverage?"

"You were already calling your press conference," she
reminded him. "I was just trying to personalize the message. Since he sent a personal one to me first."

"You're supposed to be an intelligent woman, Desiree." O'Malley leaned over her, his face inches from hers.
"Have you considered the publicity the guy would get if
he made *you* his next victim?"

No. Amazingly, she realized now with a sinking dread,
she'd never considered that possibility. Oh, there had
been that fleeting moment when she'd learned about the
ribbons, but when he hadn't contacted her again, she'd
managed to convince herself that that had only been a
coincidence.

"I guess I should have thought it through more carefully," she admitted. The problem was ever since meeting Roman, she'd been reckless, and look where it had
led—to a dangerous mistake.

"You should have been more careful," he said. "Hell,
Desiree, I don't want to scare you, but—"

"Yes, you do."

He rubbed his chin as he considered that. "You're right.
I guess I do. But it's only because I care about what happens to you."

"I know." She had a sudden urge to wrap her arms around him and press her cheek against his broad chest. But knowing that she no longer had the right, she refrained from any physical contact.

"I want to put a man on you."

"A bodyguard?"

"Just until this guy is caught."

"That could be a very long time."

"Perhaps."

"Or perhaps not?" she suggested, instantly alert at his tone. No longer a woman concerned for her own safety, she'd switched into her reporter mode. "Are you saying you've got a lead on him?"

"This is off the record."

"So what isn't with you?" she said with resignation.

"The florist is down at headquarters right now, working with a police artist on a composite. We also have an eye witness who saw him pick up the girl in the Santa's helper outfit."

"Are you saying your witness can actually identify him?" This was a break.

"Not the guy, unfortunately. But he did manage to identify the make of the car, although he didn't get the plate numbers. We're running a check of all the black Porches licensed in the parish."

"He drives a black Porsche?" An image flashed through Desiree's mind. An image of Roman Falconer emerging from the dark sports car parked at the curb outside her house.

It was only a coincidence, she told herself, just as she'd done when she heard about the rapist seeming to have read her book. There was no way she was possibly going to believe that the man who'd made her tea and covered her with the soft wool afghan she'd bought during last year's vacation with O'Malley to his ancestral home in County Wexford could possibly be a vicious, mentally deranged killer.

"Black or dark blue. Even with the Christmas lights at the entrance to the park, it was a little hard to tell."

"There must be a lot of Porsches in Orleans Parish. How are you going to run them all down?"

"One at a time."

"You'll find him," Desiree said, knowing that this man more than most had the patience required to do exactly that.

"Not standing around here, I won't." He reached out as if to run his hand down her face, then withdrew it. "I'd better go."

"Yes." She was tired of keeping her distance. Perhaps he didn't believe former lovers could be friends, but she was damned if she was going to pretend that she didn't still have feelings. "Thanks for caring, O'Malley." She went up on her toes and kissed his cheek.

A dark flush rose from his collar and he quickly looked around, as if half expecting to see Karyn standing in the kitchen.

"A Christmas kiss between friends, O'Malley. That's all it was," Desiree said with a grin.

He returned her grin, looking as if she'd taken a load off his shoulders. "In that case—" he bent his head and brushed a light kiss against her smiling lips "—Merry Christmas to you, too."

The kiss was warm and sweet and failed to stimulate so much as a tinge of desire. Relieved, Desiree allowed her lips to cling and thought how strange it was that she had the French Quarter rapist to thank for bringing this warm and caring man back into her life.

"About that bodyguard," she said as the brief kiss ended.

"It's not up for discussion. He's outside now. And he'll stay with you until the rapist is behind bars."

"He'll interfere with my work."

"Tough." This time he allowed his hand to sweep up her cheek. "Protect and serve, remember?"

Despite the tender touch, the no-nonsense detective was back. In spades. Oh well, Desiree thought as she watched O'Malley stop to talk to the man in the unmarked sedan parked across the street, she was a clever woman.

If the bodyguard O'Malley had saddled her with became a hindrance, she'd just have to figure out some way to ditch him.

11

AFTER RELUCTANTLY returning home, Roman rewound the video tape, then punched play on the remote with more force than was necessary. It was the fifth time he'd watched Desiree's report, and unfortunately, it didn't get a damn bit better with repetition. She was either the most daring or the most foolish woman he'd ever had the misfortune to meet.

But now that their paths *had* crossed, he had no choice.

Since fate had dropped Desiree Dupree into his life, it was up to him to do something about her. Before she managed to make things even worse than they already were.

"Fat chance of that."

He blackened the television screen, picked up the Scotch bottle from the table beside the chair and refilled his glass. The glass was almost to his lips when, on an afterthought, he carried the bottle and the glass into the kitchen and poured the contents down the sink. Then he went around the house, retrieving other bottles from other rooms.

He had plans to make. And in order to pull them off, he needed to be stone-cold sober.

DESIREE WAS NOT in the best of moods when she returned to the station after the press conference. Other than stating the make and color of the alleged rapist's car and assuring the gathered members of the press that the police were on top of the case and expected an arrest soon, O'Malley hadn't given her any solid facts to work with.

At this point, since they hadn't yet identified the dead girl—who was, it was assumed, another prostitute—Desiree couldn't even try to track down family members. She'd interviewed some of the girls on the street, hoping to learn something about the victim. But the rapes—and now the murder—had everyone edgy.

Add to that the silent shadow that had not let her out of his sight, and Desiree was not surprised when not a single one of the prostitutes had proved cooperative.

"I can't get a slant on this story," she complained.

"When in doubt as to your target, shoot at the politicians and the police," Adrian suggested.

They were in his office, working on her evening report. Someone had adorned the wood-paneled office with garlands of gold tinsel in an attempt to add holiday cheer. A wreath fashioned of red chili peppers, the kind used to make Louisiana's famous hot Tabasco sauce, adorned the window that looked out over the sidewalk.

"Hit them between their myopic, bureaucratic eyes for not releasing the facts about the guy sooner," he instructed, building up steam as he lit a cigarette and ignoring, as he always did, the station's no-smoking policy.

"I already addressed their failure to warn people in my morning report," she reminded him. "I need something new. Something more visual. This is, after all, photojournalism."

He leaned back in his chair, breathed out a cloud of blue smoke and gazed thoughtfully out the festooned window at the shoppers crowding Royal Street. "It's too bad the guy hasn't responded to your offer. It's not that he hasn't had a chance. We've been running the spot as a newsbreak all day."

"I know. O'Malley's about to blow his stack."

"If he'd caught the guy sooner, there wouldn't be anything for him to get pissed off about." He dragged a hand through his thinning hair. "The stuff Sugar's already shot at the cemetery and the pond will still work," he decided. "Intermixing those with shots of all the holiday tourists and using a voice-over should stir people up."

"I don't want to just stir people up. That's what programs like *Hard Copy* and *A Current Affair* like to do. What about enlightening and informing our viewers?"

"Fine, to a point," he agreed. "But if we don't keep our ratings up, Des, we won't have any viewers left *to* inform. Let's not forget that it's the sizzle that sells the steak."

He was, of course, right. But there were times, and this was one of them, when Desiree was forced to acknowledge how very thin a line there was between legitimate news and the ever-growing, increasingly popular tabloid journalism.

"Perhaps I'll go back to the park," she suggested, "and see if I can find out any more information on those kids who discovered her body."

"Great idea," he agreed enthusiastically. "Especially if they're good-looking. The fact that they were making out at the time adds to the appeal. Lord, talk about throwing cold water on teenage passion!"

Desiree rolled her eyes. "You're such an inspiration, Adrian."

"I do my best," he said easily, ignoring her dry tone. The intercom on his desk buzzed, signaling a call. "This'll probably be for sales," he muttered.

A temp was filling in for the receptionist, who'd left yesterday for Nashville to visit her daughter and grandchildren for Christmas. And although the new woman was friendly and eager to please, calls had been misrouted all day.

He punched the speaker button. "What is it now, Charlene?"

"Mr. Beauvier? Is that you?"

"It's me." He exchanged a frustrated look with Desiree, who merely smiled and shrugged. "Who were you trying to reach this time?"

"You. Well, technically, I was trying to call your office." There was a pause. "The newsroom told me that Ms. Dupree is in there."

"She's sitting right here," he confirmed.

"I've got a call for her. I think it's that detective again."

He picked up the receiver and handed it to Desiree.

"Look, O'Malley," she began with a frustrated sigh, "I know you're mad, but—"

"I saw your report this morning," a deep, husky voice that carried the unmistakable cadence of the bayou interrupted. "You are not only an extremely beautiful woman, Ms. Dupree, you're very talented, as well."

There was something about his voice. Something vaguely sinister. "Who is this?" Desiree demanded.

"That's not important. What *is* important is that I want you to know I appreciate your offer."

"Offer?"

She rubbed her suddenly throbbing temple and turned toward the glass window that looked out over the newsroom. There, on her desk, the phone O'Malley's detectives had tapped sat idle. Damn! How could she have made such a stupid mistake? Of course, the regular receptionist would have remembered to route all calls to her private line.

"Your generous invitation to accompany me to the police station, of course. So those thugs wouldn't harm me."

He didn't sound like a crazed killer, she realized as she madly scribbled a note for Adrian to pick up an extension.

"Are you saying you're the French Quarter rapist?" That was all it took to send the producer racing from the room. She watched as he stopped at her desk and carefully picked up the receiver.

"Of course. Were you expecting Charles Manson?" He laughed at his own feeble joke.

"You know," she said with a great deal more aplomb than she was feeling, "you aren't the first person to confess to a crime you didn't commit. How do I know you're really him?"

"Ah, this is where you want me to tell you something private. Something only the rapist would know."

"That would help prove your authenticity."

"How about the ribbons? The scarlet ribbons. Such a pretty color, don't you think?" His voice dropped even lower and turned unnervingly intimate. It was a cross between a purr and a growl, and it made her flesh crawl. "And appropriate for the season, being so festive."

"That's a rather ironic thing for you to say," she couldn't help replying. "Killing a girl in a Santa Claus-helper suit wasn't exactly festive."

"That was a mistake." She heard a flare of temper, which he immediately controlled. "She shouldn't have fought so hard. A little resistance adds spice to the encounter—" he paused and sighed loudly "—but she should not have fought so hard."

Desiree closed her eyes in pain as she thought about the young girl's last, tragic moments of life. "Look, we really do have to talk." She was determined to do whatever she could to get this dangerous, psychotic man off the streets.

"And we will," he agreed, his tone once again turning smooth and silky. It was a voice of a man accustomed to charming women. It was also, she reminded herself, the voice of a man who killed them. "But not right now. Not when there's a very good chance that O'Malley has tapped this line. Goodbye, Ms. Dupree. Until next time, *Joyeux Noël.*"

"Wait—"

There was a click. Then the steady drone of a dial tone.

"Damn, damn, damn!" Desiree was on her feet, pacing the floor, her mind whirling as she chastised herself for having picked up the wrong line and, even worse, let him get away without her having a clue as to his identity.

Her producer was not nearly so demonstrative. "Well," he said in an accent similar to the one belonging to her caller, "looks as if you've got tonight's lead."

Desiree was exhausted and more than a little cranky when she finally arrived home after the late newscast. Unsurprisingly, O'Malley had not been at all thrilled by the news that she'd spoken with the caller on an untapped line. The way he'd grilled her—someone he had once professed to love—seemingly for hours made her wonder what he was like when interrogating murderers.

Which her caller was, she reminded herself as she pulled her car into her driveway. As wrapped up in her news story as she was, she couldn't forget that a serial rapist and murderer had singled her out for attention.

"Not that O'Malley would let me forget," she muttered as she cast a glance into the rearview mirror and spotted her shadow pulling the sedan into his regular spot across the street. A street that was especially dark due to the streetlight in front of her house having obviously been broken since last night.

As she climbed out of her car, she saw a man emerge from the shadows toward her. Even as fear skimmed up her spine she heard the door on the unmarked patrol car open. A moment later, she recognized the familiar face.

"What are you doing here?"

"I brought you a tree," Roman said, as if there was nothing at all unusual in the gesture.

"A tree?"

"A Christmas tree."

"Oh." She glanced past him, at his car, recognizing the shadowy shape that had been tied to the top. The cop was now less than five feet away, his hand beneath his leather jacket.

"It's all right, Officer," she assured him. "It's not the man you're looking for."

"Are you certain?" He glanced at the black Porsche, which was almost swallowed by the night, as he pulled out his police-issue 9 mm pistol. "The car's the same as the one on the APB."

"Nevertheless, Mr. Falconer is a friend of mine." That wasn't precisely true. The chemistry they'd experienced from the beginning had little to do with friendship. Still, Desiree considered, he *had* made her tea last night. And covered her with a quilt when she'd fallen asleep.

"Mr. Falconer?" The cop came closer. "Hey, it *is* you." As Desiree watched, he visibly relaxed his rigid, on-duty stance and returned the ugly black pistol to its shoulder holster beneath his jacket. "You're right about it being okay," he told Desiree. "Mr. Falconer used to be one of us."

With that recommendation, he turned and walked back to the car.

"It's nice to be remembered," Roman murmured.

"A district attorney with a ninety-seven percent conviction rate is bound to have friends at the cop shop."

"Sounds as if you've been checking up on me." Roman wondered if her interest had been personal or professional.

"It's my job to check up on people," she reminded him as she turned and began walking toward her front door.

"Sounds good to me." His smile was a friendly slash of white, with none of its usual sardonic overtones. "So, how about the tree?"

Growing up with her grandmother had taught Desiree that no gift ever came without strings. "Why on earth would you bring me a Christmas tree?"

"Because unless you've gone shopping since last night, you don't have one."

"You don't, either." Or he hadn't, when she'd been at his house. And from the gloomy mood that had hung over the place like a shroud, she wouldn't have expected him to.

"I figured you might let me share yours."

His tone was unrelentingly and uncharacteristically upbeat. She leaned forward, damning whatever rotten, adolescent monster had broken the streetlight. If she could only see his face better . . .

"I don't have any ornaments."

Childhood Christmases spent alone at boarding school, with only the staff for company while her classmates were home with their families, had never been a happy time for Desiree. Unfortunately, those rare

Christmases she'd spent in New Orleans with Olivia Porter had proved even worse. That being the case, Desiree saw no reason to go overboard celebrating the season that others seemed to get so excited about.

Once, during her sophomore year in college, she'd driven out to the bayou to visit her father's family—the dozens of aunts and uncles, and the cousins who, if things had been different, she would have grown up with. But she could tell that the expensive presents she'd brought them, professionally wrapped in gilt paper and silver ribbons, had made them uncomfortable.

And although she was nothing like her grandmother, she could tell that they considered her more Porter than Dupree. The gulf that had grown between them during the decade-long separation had proved too wide and too deep to breach.

So, having no family to spend the holidays with, she wrote generous checks to several charities, brought cookies to the station Christmas party, contributed a Barbie doll with extensive accessories and clothes to the marines' toy drive and did her stint, along with other members of the news crew, dishing up a hot meal at one of the city's many homeless shelters. That was about all the festivities she could handle.

"I stopped at Santa's Quarters on my way over here and picked up some ornaments," he said with the persistence of a telemarketing salesman. "Just in case you didn't have any."

First a Christmas tree. Now ornaments. This was getting curiouser and curiouser. "Exactly how much have you had to drink?" she asked suspiciously.

"Not a single drop all day."

They'd reached her front porch. Desiree studied him intently in the yellow glow of her porch light and decided that about this, at least, he seemed to be telling the truth.

"I really am exhausted."

"I'm not surprised, considering the hours you've put in today. But you're in luck, because I'm a dynamite tree trimmer. You don't have to do a thing but sit on the sofa, sip eggnog and tell me whether on not the angel at the top of the tree is on straight."

"I don't have any eggnog."

"Ah, but I do."

"Gee, you don't look like Papa Noël."

He slanted her his most appealing smile. "Appearances can often be deceiving."

And she was definitely an example of that. Although she looked as soft and delicate as the angel hair his mother used to put on their family Christmas tree, he'd already discovered that the lady was a helluva lot tougher than she looked.

Even as tired as Desiree was, the scenario Roman was describing was admittedly appealing. And tempting. Too tempting, perhaps.

She realized this was the second time they'd been together that she actually felt comfortable with him. The previous time had been over dinner, right before Adrian had called about the rapist's latest victim.

"Don't think about him," Roman said softly. "Not tonight."

"I don't know who you're talking about."

"Of course you do." He'd watched the color fade from her cheeks. Seen the shadow move into her eyes. "The creep's on everyone's mind these days. But, hey, it's Christmas." He took both her hands in his. "A time of peace on earth, goodwill toward men. A time of joy, of mistletoe and merriment, of Dasher and Dancer, and Rudolph, and—"

"I get it." Desiree laughed and shook her head, both confused and charmed by this change in Roman.

"Did I happen to mention that I also picked up some fudge from Laura's?"

Laura's Original Praline and Fudge Shoppe was New Orleans's oldest candy store, located not far from the station. Desiree had often sworn that she could gain ten pounds just walking past the building and breathing in the rich aroma.

"Not the kind with pecans." Although the store specialized in seven varieties of pralines and was famous for its hand-dipped chocolates, Desiree's personal favorite was the sinfully rich pecan-studded dark fudge.

Roman grinned. "Is there any other kind?"

She could feel herself giving in, as she suspected he'd known all along she would. "I don't understand. What happened to you, anyway? Did the Ghost of Christmas Past show up and turn your life around?"

More like the Ghost of Christmas Present, he could have answered. A present that had grown so dark and so terrifying, he knew that if he didn't allow himself this brief respite from the horrors that had taken hold of his mind, he'd go mad.

"Nothing that dramatic." He lifted their joined hands to his lips and brushed a light kiss against her knuckles. "We got off to a bad start, Desiree. Which I'll readily admit was entirely my fault. And now I'm trying to atone for my bad behavior."

Although the cold front had blessedly blown eastward out of the city, the night was still cool. When the brief, unthreatening touch of his lips against her hand warmed her skin, Desiree reminded herself that Roman was an intensely complicated man. As much as she wanted to, she couldn't quite trust his sudden change in attitude.

"What you're trying to do is get me into bed."

"That, too." He flashed her an unrepentant grin that was surprisingly boyish. And, heaven help her, infinitely appealing. "You're an extremely attractive woman, Desiree. Any man in his right mind would want to make love with you. But for now, why don't we just start with the tree, take things nice and slow, and if we end up together in bed, it will be because we both want to be there."

It sounded reasonable. Rational. Even as a faint warning voice tried to make itself heard in the back of her mind, Desiree threw in the towel. "I think I might like a tree," she admitted.

"I was hoping you'd say that."

As she watched him jog back to the Porsche, Desiree felt a surge of something that felt remarkably like anticipation, and suddenly realized that she was not nearly as tired as she'd first thought.

Given the compact size of her house, she figured that Roman would have purchased a small, tidy little tree that would fit on a table.

But no. Like everything else about the man—like Roman himself—the towering blue spruce was larger than life.

"Don't you do anything halfway?" she asked two hours later. She was sitting on the couch as he'd promised, her feet tucked underneath her as she sipped the nutmeg-garnished eggnog he'd poured into glass mugs. "That looks like the Christmas tree that ate New Orleans."

He turned from putting a blown-glass ornament on an upper limb. "You don't like it?" he asked, looking down at her from the tall ladder. Although he'd been forced to cut two feet off the bottom of the spruce, the top was still touching the ten-foot ceiling.

"It's lovely." Actually, it was better than lovely, it was the most perfect tree she'd ever seen in her life. "It's just a little large."

"It looked smaller surrounded by all those other trees." He backed down the ladder and observed the evergreen, covered in exquisite, handmade ornaments and twinkling white lights. "I guess I did kind of overdo it."

His disappointed look was so far removed from the scowl she'd grown accustomed to seeing on his rugged face that Desiree felt the last of her resistance melting away.

"When I was a little girl, I dreamed of having a tree like this," she admitted softly.

"Really?" Roman was pleased that he'd finally managed to do something right where this woman was concerned. "I would have thought your grandmother would have had professionals come in to decorate each year."

Not that any of the neighbors would have been invited in to see the results, he realized, remembering that Olivia Porter had been the only resident of Audubon Place who'd refused to open her door to the neighborhood carolers each year.

"She did." Desiree sighed and ran her finger around the rim of her mug. "But she never let them use a real tree—the needles get in the carpet."

"I guess that explains that stainless-steel monstrosity gracing her front window every year."

Desiree grinned, glad to find someone who'd found the tree as hideous as she had. "Don't forget the rotating colored spotlights."

"Ah yes, the spotlights." He returned her smile. The wicker creaked as he sat down beside her on the sofa. On the CD player, Nat King Cole was promising to be home for Christmas. "My father always said they made your grandmother's front window look like a used-car lot."

She laughed in absolute agreement. "I think I'd like your father."

"I know he'd love you," Roman said honestly. "In fact," he said, in an offhand way that belied the fact that he'd been working his way up to this all night, "how would you like to do me a big favor?"

Desiree was feeling more relaxed than she had in days. In weeks. In fact, if she hadn't known better, she would have thought he'd spiked the eggnog with a heavy dose of tranquilizers. "I don't see how I can refuse," she said. "After you brought me a tree."

"A big tree," he drawled, feeling pretty damn relaxed himself.

"A stunningly beautiful tree." She reached out and turned off the lamp beside the couch, displaying the towering spruce in all its sparkling glory. "I wonder if it's too late to get my house included on the Holiday Home Tour?" she asked whimsically.

The annual charity tour showcased a number of beautifully decorated homes each year. She'd covered the event her first week at the station five years ago, before moving from features to the harder-edged crime coverage she preferred.

"Funny you should mention that," he said, "because it's what I want to ask you about.... My folks are on the tour this year, and as you may know, one of the draws are the musicians and choral groups that perform at each of the stops."

She nodded, wondering where this was going.

"Well, somehow, my mother talked me into playing my sax at the damn thing. I haven't played professionally since college, and it'd be nice to have someone other than my parents around to offer a little moral support. So, what do you say?"

Desiree didn't know which she found more surprising—that Roman had once been a professional musician or that he was so willing to put himself in the spotlight for his mother.

"I think I'm speechless."

He put his arm casually, unthreateningly, around her shoulders. "Just say yes."

This easy going man wearing faded blue jeans, a Tulane sweatshirt and scuffed cowboy boots, who'd brought her a tree and eggnog and even that corny batch of Christmas CDs, was unrecognizable from the man she'd found hiding away in that dark and dreary house.

"Tell me the truth, what have you done with the real Roman Falconer?" she demanded, not quite jokingly.

"You're looking at him."

"So who was that other guy lurking around your house? Your evil twin?"

"That's one answer," he murmured, more to himself than to her.

He sighed, telling himself that he'd been a fool to think he could just turn things around without some kind of explanation. The problem was, in order to explain to Desiree what had been happening to him, he'd have to understand it himself. Which he damn well didn't.

He took her hand. "I owe you an apology. I haven't been at my best lately." That was the understatement of a lifetime. "But I promise to improve."

She glanced down at their linked hands and thought how right they looked together. How right they felt. "May I ask what brought about this change of heart?" She still couldn't quite get a handle on Roman, still suspected that there was something he wasn't telling her.

"I don't suppose you'd believe that I was suddenly infused with an overdose of holiday cheer?"

"I saw your holiday cheer, remember? And it was 80 proof."

"You're a tough cookie, Desiree Dupree." His hands framed her face as his eyes met hers.

"I've had to be."

He considered that for a moment. "I suppose so." She hadn't been the only one doing a little digging into the past. He'd gone to the *Picayune*'s morgue and retrieved all the files about her parent's deaths and the tragic custody battle that her father's sister had lost before it had begun.

Although he suspected she'd hate him for suggesting it, and hate him even more for pitying her, Desiree was the quintessential poor little rich girl.

"Look, if you don't want to come, fine," he said with a nonchalant attitude he was a very long way from feeling. "But I'd feel better if you were there. And I think you might actually enjoy yourself."

Having always prided herself on her ability to make quick decisions, Desiree made one now.

"I've always wanted to date a musician," she said with a soft, lilting laugh that reminded Roman of silver bells and made him think that, just perhaps, things might actually be looking up.

12

ONLY SCROOGE or the Grinch could have refused to get in the Christmas spirit in such a splendid setting, Desiree decided as she sipped champagne and admired the lushly decorated rooms of the Falconer mansion. A striking amalgamation of the Italianate and Greek Revival architectural styles that had been popular in New Orleans in the last half of the nineteenth century, the spacious house was resplendently dressed for the holidays.

White candles glowed warmly, wreaths hung in every window, fragrant green swags had been wrapped around the banisters of the exquisite, double floating staircase, more garlands adorned mantles and every room boasted an ornately decorated tree of southern pine, wax myrtle or blue spruce.

The guests were as eclectic as the house itself. There was the usual mix of tourists, in town for the holidays, who'd undoubtedly read about the tour in their hotel magazine guide. Dressed in everything from silk to denim, they oohed and aahed appreciatively at the grandeur of their surroundings.

In addition, there were the locals, as well as most of the Falconers' Audubon Place neighbors, who'd dressed as if for a party, which indeed it was. Carolers, costumed to look as if they'd just stepped off the pages of *A Christmas Carol*, strolled through the rooms singing seasonal madrigals, while in the huge front parlor, beside a towering, sixteen-foot tree decorated with angels, gold bows and musical instruments, Roman joined a jazz band, playing a spicy version of "White Christmas" on his alto sax.

Dressed again in black tie, he was every bit as striking as he'd been the night of the charity auction. But tonight he was visibly more relaxed. He smiled often and easily, and his jet hair was mussed in a way that made a woman want to comb her hands through it.

He'd loosened his tie and unfastened the top button of his pleated white dress shirt. When she found herself wanting to unfasten a few more of those ebony studs, Desiree curled her fingers more tightly around the stem of her champagne glass to keep them out of trouble.

After the song ended, Roman exchanged a few words with the other musicians. A rakish grin spread across his face, revealing a deep dimple she'd never noticed before in his left cheek. His gaze swept the room, looking for someone. When he found Desiree, he gave her a bold wink.

"Gracious," a woman standing next to her said as he shrugged out of his jacket and tossed it atop the gleaming concert grand piano. "I wonder how good a girl you have to be to have Santa leave that hunk of a sax player under your pillow."

"He's a very good musician," Desiree said mildly, tamping down the urge to assure the woman that Roman was taken.

"I wasn't talking about his horn playing, honey." The woman, clad in a short, scarlet silk dress that proved an attractive foil for her café au lait complexion, shot a quick, unbelieving glance Desiree's way. "I was talking about those dark and dangerous looks."

"I suppose he is rather good-looking," Desiree admitted.

"Rather good-looking?" the woman echoed. "Girl-friend, if that's as good as you can do, you need a new dictionary. Or a pair of glasses."

What she was in need of was a bit of fresh air, Desiree decided as the band broke into a raucous, juiced-up version of "Jingle Bells" with a blues twist, a performance was proving to be as sexy to watch as any MTV video. The crowd in the double parlor—especially the women—went wild.

She made her way through the throng of enthusiastic party goers and slipped out a side door that led onto a covered veranda. A soft rain had begun to fall, blurring the fairy lights sparkling like starlight in the oak trees. It was a night made for romance.

It had been a long time since Desiree had let herself think about anything but her work. But when Roman had arrived at her house this evening, looking sexier than any man had a right to, he'd set off a wild flapping of wings in her stomach. And not just your usual run-of-the-mill butterflies. Oh, no. These babies were gigantic, like the huge blue egrets she remembered from the bayou. As a little girl, she'd sat in her daddy's pirogue as they glided through the silent dark waters, amazed that such large, long-legged birds could actually fly.

The memory, like all her others about those carefree, youthful days, was bittersweet. After all these years, she still missed her parents, especially at this time of year.

She was looking out over the lush green lawn that could have doubled as a putting green when she felt Roman come up behind her. She did not need to turn around; it was as if she'd developed a second sense that told her whenever he was in the vicinity.

"I was hoping I'd find you out here." His voice was deep and warm and every bit as smooth as the fudge he'd brought her last night. Although Desiree had always considered herself a fairly strong-willed individual, she'd not been able to resist that luscious sweet candy. Just as she was finding it impossible to resist this man.

"It was beginning to feel a bit crowded in there," she murmured. When he looped his arms around her waist, she instinctively leaned back against his chest.

"And hot," he agreed. "The place is packed. I can't believe how many people showed up."

"That undoubtedly has a great deal to do with word getting out that you were going to be part of the entertainment."

"I suppose people like to watch so-called celebrities make fools of themselves."

"You didn't make a fool of yourself. Actually," she confessed, "I was surprised at how good you are."

"Oh, I've got all sorts of hidden talents."

Desiree, who had no doubt of that, didn't answer.

Roman rested his chin atop her head and drank in her scent. "Did I mention that you look exceptionally beautiful tonight?"

"When you first showed up at my house."

"Well, it bears repeating. That's a gorgeous dress. Sexy and classy at the same time."

"It belonged to my mother. When my grandmother died last autumn, I was cleaning out her house and discovered it packed away in white tissue paper in an old steamer trunk in her attic."

A fluid column of bronze silk, the long gown caressed Desiree's slender curves. The high, beaded neckline of the halter top kept the front of the dress modest while the back dipped to the waist, revealing a weakening amount of creamy flesh. When he had an almost overwhelming urge to press his lips against that smooth white expanse of bare skin, Roman knew he was losing it.

"Although I'm no expert on women's fashion, I think it could have been designed with you in mind." He pushed aside her thick hair, giving his lips access to her earlobe.

Desiree drew in an expectant breath as he tugged off one of her earrings. The diamond-and-yellow-sapphire star bursts, like the evening gown, had belonged to her mother—the only things Katherine Porter had taken when she'd left her mother's home to elope with Lucky Dupree. The earrings could have solved a great many financial problems during those lean years, but Lucky had been a proud man. He'd steadfastly refused to allow his wife to sell the precious jewelry, even when the fishing was light and the traps came up empty more times than full.

Knowing enough not to argue with her husband and loving him too much to challenge his chauvinism, Katherine instead would don the sparkling star bursts every Christmas, never minding that they were definitely overkill for the bayou.

Desiree's neck was slender and pale in the glow from the twinkling white Christmas lights. The mysteriously exotic scent he'd not been able to get out of his mind for days drifted up from that soft flesh, clouding his mind. "Lord, I love the way you smell."

When his teeth closed over her earlobe, she closed her eyes. When his lips skimmed down the side of her neck, she trembled.

Observing her slight shiver, Roman plucked his jacket from where he'd laid it over the wrought-iron railing and placed it on her shoulders. "Perhaps we ought to go back in."

Desiree offered no resistance as he turned her in his arms. His husky tone suggested that returning to the noisy public rooms was not his first choice.

"If that's what you want."

He drew her closer. "Hell no, it's not what I want."

What he wanted was to scoop her into his arms, carry her up his mother's beloved Caroline stairway to the nearest bedroom and ravish every inch of her smooth, perfumed and powdered flesh. When she shivered again, he managed, just barely, to stamp down the urge to follow his instincts. "But you're cold."

"Actually," she admitted with a breathless little laugh, "I think I'm burning up."

His laugh was rough, half relief, half frustration. "Do you have any idea what it does to me when you look at me like that?" He ran the back of his hand down the side of her face. "When you say things like that to me?"

Desiree linked her hands together around his neck. "Why don't you show me?"

"With pleasure." His hands moved down her back, settling on her hips, pressing her against him. "How's this for starters?" he asked as his lips plucked seductively at hers.

"Not bad." She moved against him, creating friction, sparking heat. "For starters."

"You keep moving against me like that, sweetheart," he growled, "and I won't be responsible for the consequences."

Instead of backing away, she pressed even closer, thrilled by the feel of his hard male body against hers. "Is that a threat or a promise?"

Roman had promised himself that he wouldn't rush things. That he'd take his time, slipping past her emotional barricades with easy words and affectionate touches. But as his mouth claimed hers, he realized that there was nothing easy where this woman was concerned. The hard truth was that he wanted her. Desperately. He wanted her lying beneath him. Naked. Writhing. Screaming.

They came together like thunder. Like lightning. The passion he'd managed to cage that night on the dance floor tore through him.

Every coherent thought Desiree had possessed was scattered to the hot winds swirling around them. There was only here. Only now. Only Roman.

When he stroked a silk-covered breast with his palm, she gasped in heated response, allowing him to plunder the dark recesses of her mouth with his tongue.

His knee slipped between her legs, pressing against her, creating a warm moisture to pool between her thighs. His hands were everywhere—on her hair, her breasts, her hips—leaving fire wherever they touched, creating soft moans born not of pain, but of tormented pleasure.

Drunk with passion, she dragged her fingers through his hair, her avid mouth restlessly trying to recapture his lips as they streaked over her face, leaving stinging kisses against her cheeks, her temples, her jaw.

There was a violence in him. A savage, primal passion that thrilled Desiree even as it made her tremble. His jacket slid off her shoulders, falling unnoticed to the flagstone. She heard his name over and over again, half moan, half plea, and realized through her burning senses that the sound was coming from her own lips.

Needs pounded through Roman, bombarding his senses, scorching away his earlier vow of restraint.

Through the roaring in his head, he realized that one taste of Desiree would never be enough. He wanted to devour her—her warm ripe mouth; her hot skin, which was practically melting beneath his desperately roving hands; her bones.

Because he was dangerously close to taking her here and now, on his parents' flagstone terrace, he managed, just barely, to curb the beast clawing inside him and grasp onto one faint, lingering thread of civilized behavior.

Too fast, he told himself as he dragged his mouth from hers. Fueled by his own burning hunger, driven by her uninhibited response, he'd allowed himself to rush things. To take, when what he wanted to do was to give.

"Lord, lady, do you have any idea how much I want you?"

His forehead was on hers. His breath was rough and ragged and his hands, as they returned to her waist, were far from steady.

"Yes." As she felt him garnering control, Desiree discovered that it was possible to feel relief and regret at the same time. "Because I want you, too, Roman. Too much for comfort. Too much for safety."

"Neither of us have been safe since that first night." His cooling body continued to throb painfully as he looked down into her open face and saw both vulnerability and independence. It was, he'd come to realize since meeting her, an irresistible combination.

When she didn't immediately answer, he took one of her hands, which were now pressed against the front of his shirt, and lifted it to his lips. "Let's go back to your place for a nightcap."

The flame still burning in his dark, hypnotic eyes told Desiree that he was suggesting a lot more than a bit of spiked eggnog or brandy.

As his teeth scraped seductively at her knuckles, she gasped softly. "Oh, yes." Her usually modulated voice was every bit as unsteady as his.

He exhaled a long deep breath, feeling like a man who'd just made the decision to leap off the edge of a very steep and perilous precipice. There was, he knew, no going back.

He framed her face with his palms and gave her a long, inscrutable look. Then he kissed her. This time he was unbearably gentle and amazingly patient. Still, her mind clouded.

"There's something you need to know," she said when the blissful kiss finally ended.

"What's that?" He turned her hand, which he still held, pressed his lips against her unreasonably delicate wrist and felt her pulse leap.

"I don't take sex lightly." She bit her lip, worrying that she was sounding horribly unsophisticated. Which, in truth, she was. Other than a boy she'd thought she loved in college, who'd left her for a woman whose parents summered in Newport Beach and whose grandfather could buy him a seat on the New York Stock Exchange, Michael had been the only other man she'd ever made love with. "I wish I could." Her eyes were wide and sober, asking him to understand. "But I can't."

"Believe me, Desiree, I don't take anything about you lightly." He brushed her reddened lower lip with the pad of his thumb, the caressing touch both soothing and exciting at the same time. "I wish I could."

Roman sighed, worried that he was about to make the biggest mistake of his life. Unable to stop himself, he could only hope that it didn't also turn out to be the biggest mistake of hers.

"Let's get out of here. Before I get talked into playing another chorus of 'Sleigh Ride.'"

Her heart shining in her eyes, Desiree laughed her acquiescence.

Unfortunately, escape did not prove all that easy. They'd almost made their way to the door when a tall, slender, dark-haired woman clad in a gold crepe dress stepped in front of them.

"Darling!" With a smile as dazzling as the diamonds glistening like ice at her ears, she framed Roman's face in her hands. "You can't leave before I thank you for a marvelous performance." She kissed him on the cheek, then rubbed at the vermillion spot with her fingertips before turning to Desiree. "I'm sorry. I'm not usually so rude, but it's not all that often I can convince my son to play in public."

She held out a slim hand. More diamonds sparkled, and rubies gleamed on long manicured fingers. "Hello, Desiree, dear. It's so good to see you again."

"Hello, Mrs. Falconer. Your home is beautiful."

"The decorations turned out well, didn't they?" Margaret Falconer glanced around the parlor with satisfaction. Her bright, dancing gaze returned for a judicious study of the first young female her son had ever invited to her home. "You've certainly grown into a lovely woman, Desiree." She slanted a pleased look at her silent son. "Hasn't she, Roman?"

"Stunning." His husky tone, along with the blatant hunger stamped onto that face she knew so well, told Margaret exactly what she wanted to know.

"Of course, it's no surprise that you're a beauty," Margaret continued, "since you look exactly like your mother."

"You knew my mother?"

"Of course. Katherine and I were best friends all through school." A smooth brow furrowed. "You didn't know that?"

"No." Desiree shook her head, confused by the unexpected anger she thought she saw flash in Margaret Falconer's dark eyes. "Mother didn't talk about her life in New Orleans."

"I'm not surprised." There was an edge to her tone that reminded Desiree of Roman's voice when he turned coldly furious. "It wasn't a very happy life. But later, when you came to live with Olivia, there were several times over the years when I invited you to the house. I thought you might like to talk about your mother."

"Oh, I *would* have liked that." So much, Desiree thought. Especially since her grandmother had not permitted Katherine Porter Dupree's name to be spoken in her presence.

"Whenever I asked, your grandmother insisted you wanted nothing to do with any of your mother's old friends." Roman's mother sighed and shook her head sadly. "Obviously, she was lying."

"Yes." Having expected nothing from her grandmother, such selfish treachery shouldn't disappoint. But it did. "Obviously."

"Well, then," Margaret said with the decisiveness that had made her, before she'd turned to teaching at Tulane, a very successful litigator, "better late than never. Why don't we have a long lunch at The Court of the Two Sisters next week?"

Desiree didn't know whether to burst into tears or kiss Roman's mother. In the end, she did neither, agreeing to the surprise luncheon invitation with an enthusiasm she didn't bother to conceal.

"Your mother is a very nice woman," she said to Roman as they drove through the darkened streets. The twinkling lights on the houses they passed were reflected in the wet pavement.

"The best," he agreed easily.

He'd been surprised by the naked yearning he'd seen on Desiree's face. He also had the feeling that he could give her a deed to her very own diamond mine and still not equal his mother's gift. A lunch was not normally that big a deal, of course. Unless it was a lunch that promised to soothe more than a decade and a half of loss.

He heard Desiree's soft sigh and suspected that once again they were thinking the same thing.

"You're a lucky man."

"I guess I am." Suspecting that he took his parents for granted, Roman made a mental note to send his mother flowers first thing tomorrow morning. Well, perhaps not first thing, he reconsidered, since he'd be waking up in Desiree's bed.

A comfortable silence settled over the interior of the Porsche. Neither mentioned the unmarked sedan following discreetly behind them.

DAMN HER!

The man in black had stood alone in the shadows, watching Desiree kiss Roman Falconer. He'd already known that rich boy Falconer was accustomed to getting whatever he wanted. The knowledge of the district-attorney-turned-author's privileged status gnawed at the man in black's gut like battery acid.

He had his own clever scheme for dealing with that self-indulgent bastard. He'd also had plans for Desiree Dupree.

But that was before he'd discovered what a shameless slut she was. Now those plans would have to be changed.

His stomach roiled. The intense throbbing behind his eyes, the blinding pain that always came when he was upset and angry, made it difficult to think.

His carefully conceived plan was spinning out of control, dammit. Because of her.

Desiree would pay, he vowed, as he followed them down St. Charles Avenue in the car he'd stolen from outside the Falconer mansion. But not now. Not while the cacophony of voices was roaring in his head, screaming for release.

There was, he knew, only one thing that would silence them. One special, secret thing that would satiate their raging hunger.

He watched the treacherous pair enter the wanton whore's house, then drove away, headed back downtown toward his French Quarter hunting ground.

13

ALTHOUGH SHE'D KNOWN this was coming, and although she wanted very much for it to happen, Desiree found herself unreasonably nervous when they entered the house.

"Would you like a drink?" she asked.

"Not, really. But if you'd—"

"No." She shook her head. "I think I should have eaten dinner before you picked me up for the tour. That glass of champagne I had seemed to go straight to my head."

Her nerves were so tightly tangled, Roman feared they were about to snap. It wasn't going to be easy, he mused. Which was probably just as well. Although he'd grown up with wealth and privilege, he had never trusted things that came too easily.

"You should have said something." He crossed the room and turned on the tree lights. "We could have stopped for something on the way back here."

"No. I'm fine, really."

Earlier, as they'd stood among the glittering lights on the terrace, Desiree had been every bit as eager as he to leave. Her feelings about making love with Roman hadn't changed. The problem was the logistics. If she could only figure out how to get from here to the bedroom . . .

A thought flashed through her mind, a thought of Roman as some savage, Stone Age warrior, knocking her over the head with his club, then dragging her back to his cave by her hair.

"Care to share?" he asked pleasantly as he watched her luscious lips curve in a smile.

"Share?" She shook off the Neanderthal fantasy, returning to her present dilemma.

"Whatever thoughts had you smiling that way."

"Oh." She felt the color, the bane of every redhead, flow into her cheeks. "Actually, it was silly." Before he could try to pin her down, she crossed over to the CD player and began rummaging through the stack of Christmas disks he'd brought with him. "How about some music? Let's see, we have Nat King Cole. No, we did him last night. Bing Crosby—he's a classic. Oh, The Temptations should be nice, don't you think? Or..." She knew she was babbling but was unable to help herself.

She was beginning to make *him* nervous. "Desiree." Following her across the room, he took both her trembling hands in his and lifted them to his lips. "This isn't necessary." His eyes echoed his encouraging smile. "I don't need a drink. I don't need music. All I need right now is you."

"I'm sorry." She sucked in a ragged breath. "It's just that this isn't as easy as I thought it was going to be."

Roman released her hands and looped his arms lightly around her waist. "I'm not sure it should be easy." He'd known from the beginning that nothing about Desiree was going to be the slightest bit simple.

He kissed her, a soft, satiny meeting of lips, a mingling of breath. Then, as if it were the most natural thing in the world, he linked his fingers with hers and walked down the hallway to the bedroom.

It was, as he'd suspected, as lushly romantic as the rest of her Victorian cottage—an intensely feminine room where a man would feel comfortable only if invited.

The lamp had been draped in silk, creating a soft pink glow. Flowers bloomed everywhere—across the walls, on the hand-stitched rug, on the pillows piled high atop the lacy white wrought-iron bed. A rose silk moiré-covered jewel box sat atop a skirted table, the tangle of chains and gleaming cultured pearls spilling forth like a pirate's ransom. Proving both useful and decorative, antique brass hooks on the flowered walls held a selection of bright silk scarves.

A trio of antique perfume bottles adorned a wicker nightstand, along with a more modern glass jar. Roman idly opened the lid, scooped out a bit of the smooth pink cream with his finger and breathed in the familiar, haunting scent that had lingered so intensely in his mind.

Desiree watched him as he drank in the sight of her bedroom and realized she was exposing herself to him in a way that was every bit as intimate as taking off her clothes. She prided herself on her cool, collected public image, and it was only in the privacy of her own home, and most particularly here in this room, that she'd allowed her romantic fantasies free rein.

"It's you." He put the jar back onto the table.

Until that moment, when she let out the breath she'd been unaware of holding, Desiree had not realized that she'd been waiting for his approval.

"Only part of me," she insisted, inexplicably feeling the point needed to be made. "I'm an intelligent woman."

"Smart as a whip." Beside the jar of perfumed cream was a fat vanilla-scented candle and a book of matches from Broussards. He lit the candle and turned off the lamp.

"People from the governor on down to the man in the street value my opinions."

"And rightfully so." He closed the space between them in two strides.

"I've even had feelers from the network this week."

"I'm not surprised by that." The skill with which he deftly unfastened the hooks at the back of her dress revealed that this was a man who definitely knew his way around women's clothing.

"The point is . . ." She drew in a ragged breath when, with a single light touch, he sent the bronze silk skimming over her body to land in a gleaming pool at her feet. "My point is that I'm an intelligent, levelheaded . . ." She moaned softly as his lips nuzzled at her throat. "A levelheaded career woman."

"You've got a great head on these silky shoulders," he agreed, brushing his mouth over the fragrant skin in question. "A beautiful head. Have I mentioned that I love your hair? It reminds me of one of those paintings of redheaded, rosy-fleshed nudes."

When she felt her knees begin to tremble, Desiree clung to him to keep from collapsing. "I was trying to explain that I'm respected. . . ." She was determined to get the thought out before the familiar mists entirely enveloped her mind.

"I respect you." His teeth nipped at her collarbone. "Tonight." He soothed the reddened spot with the tip of his tongue. "Tomorrow morning. . . ."

When those lips moved steadily downward, to the crest of her breasts, she swayed. "Dammit, Roman," she complained, even as her fingers began ripping away at the ebony studs of his shirtfront, "I can't think when you're driving me crazy this way."

That was only fair, Roman considered, since she'd been driving him crazy from the start. "You can think later." He scooped her up in his arms and dropped her atop the white lace bedspread. "For now, just feel."

"Oh, yes." Impatient now, and stunned by how desperate hunger could be, she wrapped her arms around him, and together they rolled over the bed, ripping at clothes, desperate to touch. Demanding to be touched.

He'd wanted to give her more. He'd wanted to spend hours lingering with her, making love to her with soft kisses and slow hands. He'd planned to be infinitely patient. To tease, to tempt, to tantalize. He'd wanted to watch her float.

That had been the plan. But although he'd suspected that Desiree was a woman of great passion, he'd never imagined how deep that passion flowed.

She was hot and eager, and as greedy as he. She moved against him, under him, on top of him, touching, tasting, tormenting. Although he knew it had to be his imagination, Roman could have sworn that he smelled the smoke of hellfire mingling with her sultry scent.

"Oh, God, I absolutely love your body." She was on her knees, splendidly naked as she rained hot, stinging kisses all over his chest, his stomach, his thighs. Roman's masculine form was a fascination and a wonder to her.

Desiree loved the way his muscles rippled beneath her hands, was thrilled by the way they clenched beneath her lips. She reveled in the mysterious male taste of his moist flesh. "I've wanted it from the beginning."

"It's all yours," he managed to say with a groan, arching his back as her hair draped over his burning flesh like a silken veil.

He grabbed a handful of thick, fragrant hair and pulled, lifting her head. "You realize, of course, that you're killing me?"

Her cheeks were flushed; her eyes sparkled. "Of course." Witchlike, she laughed and touched her mouth to his, inviting him to taste himself on her lips. "I'm killing you softly," she murmured huskily, twisting the title of his latest bestseller. It was not, he thought, as she slid seductively back down his aching body, a bad way to go.

When her tongue swirled around his aching shaft, stroking it with an innate sensuality that was as much a part of her as that sprinkling of freckles on her pale white shoulders, flames shot up his spine. Fearing he was about to explode, Roman rolled her over and pressed her deeply into the mattress.

"Now."

"Now," she agreed breathlessly, twining her arms and legs around him.

As he sank into her, Roman felt her throbbing muscles contract around him, welcoming him, embracing him. He moved against her, enjoying the way her breath caught in a shuddering little hitch. He withdrew and she moaned a faint protest.

With his eyes locked on hers, he thrust deeply, causing Desiree to cry out in wonder—in triumph—as he filled her completely.

As he began to move, faster, deeper, she kept up with him, clinging to him, her fingernails digging into the flesh of his back, moving in perfect unison.

Wracked by a hard, sudden climax, her body went suddenly rigid. Roman knew he'd never seen anything more erotic as the sight of Desiree, for that suspended moment as still as a statue, her flesh gleaming like marble in the moonlight, her lips full and parted, her eyes closed in an expression of absolute ecstasy.

She cried out his name as wave after wave of pleasure washed over her.

"Desiree." Her name was ripped harshly from his throat. "Look at me."

Her lids, incredibly heavy, fluttered open.

"I want you to understand." As he fought desperately for control, Roman felt as if he were trying to hold back a raging, wild animal. "Whatever else happens, you're mine."

Blissfully exhausted, Desiree managed to grasp only the claim, missing the husky warning in his tone. Lifting arms that had turned amazingly limp, she framed his grimly set face with her palms.

"Yours." Her smile, echoed in her eyes, was beatific.

It was all he needed to hear. Roman crushed his mouth against hers and surrendered to his own release. As he poured himself into her, he realized that he'd never felt so defenseless. Or so invincible.

IT WAS A TIME of mistletoe and magic. Although she'd always considered herself a practical, feet-on-the-ground type of woman, over the next two weeks, Desiree surrendered to the season, and to Roman. As if determined to make up for all the holidays she'd missed growing up, he coaxed and cajoled her into experiencing all the joy and splendor of a true Crescent City Christmas.

Though it didn't take much persuading, she decided happily after attending a Sunday afternoon performance of Handel's *Messiah* by the New Orleans Symphony, and on the following night, a magical and delightful performance of the *Nutcracker* ballet.

Despite this dizzying, glorious time with Roman, Desiree couldn't forget that the rapist was still out there. Watching. Waiting.

"Don't think about him," Roman said, not for the first time, as they stood shoulder-to-shoulder with thousands of residents and visitors gathered together in Jackson Square for one of the season's most beloved events, Caroling in the Square.

"Who?" she asked, knowing that she could never keep anything from Roman. Once they'd both lowered their protective barriers, they'd become so close that Desiree felt as if they'd been together a lifetime, rather than fourteen short days.

"You know who." He rubbed at the line between her brows. All around them, participants had segued from "Away in a Manger" to "The First Noel." "This is our first Christmas together, Desiree. Let's not let him ruin it."

"You're right." She liked the way his words suggested that there would be more such holidays. Smiling, she rose up on her toes and, mindless of the crowd surrounding them, gave him a heartfelt kiss that promised a night of more such kisses to come.

The day before Christmas Eve they attended "Christmas in the Oaks," strolling hand-in-hand to the accompaniment of the musical groups stationed throughout City Park. Although they'd planned a sumptuous late dinner afterward at the Grill Room in the famed Windsor Court Hotel, a more insistent hunger had them skipping dinner and returning to Desiree's Victorian cottage.

By the time the candle had burned down to melted wax and the stuttering December sun was infiltrating its way past the lace covering her bedroom window, Desiree knew that she'd surrendered a great deal more than her body to Roman during these festive days and nights. She'd also given him her heart.

"I may never move again." She cuddled against him, her smiling lips against his chest, her legs entwined with his.

"I could live with that." He ran his hand down her hair, picking up a few strands and holding them to the light, enjoying the way the sunlight turned them to copper and gold.

"Of course, we might starve."

"Never happen." He kissed her smiling lips and knew he'd never been happier. Or more terrified. These past days and nights, as glorious as they had been, had been wrapped in the seductive golden glow of the holiday season. Soon, in the bright, unforgiving light of a new day, they were both going to have to face some unpleasant facts that could destroy everything. "We'll live on love."

As he ran his hand down her back, incredibly, after all they'd shared, she felt the shimmering heat rising once more. "Oh, I think I really, really like that idea."

Although she'd been expecting the tenderness he'd displayed so many times, his next kiss was harsh and strangely desperate.

"I do, you know," he said when the kiss ended.

"Do what?" There was something in his eyes. Something dark and tragic. Something that reminded her of that haunted man she'd first seen outside the cemetery.

"Love you."

Both pleased and confused, she studied his grim expression. "You don't exactly sound thrilled by the idea."

"I want to be."

She felt the pleasure slipping away, like sand between her fingers. "But?"

"It's not that simple."

She surprised him by smiling—a tender smile that had the power to take his breath away. "Nothing worth having ever is." It was her turn to kiss him, and although her lips lingered, she kept her touch light. And reassuring. "Why don't I fix some coffee?" she suggested. "And heat up some rolls. We can have breakfast in bed. And talk."

Talking was the last thing he wanted to do with this woman. But Roman knew he'd put this conversation off far too long already. His answering kiss was quick and hot. "You're right."

"Right?" She pressed her fingers against her tingling lips. "About what?"

"You *are* an intelligent woman."

"Well, of course." Her grin was quick and lively and made her eyes gleam. "I already told you that."

She reluctantly slipped from beneath the sheets, feeling no shame as she watched Roman watching her. "If you keep looking at me like that, I'm going to forget about the coffee," she threatened with a breathless little laugh.

Before he could answer, the phone beside the bed rang. At the same time the doorbell chimed.

"You get the phone," he said, retrieving his slacks from the floor and pulling them on. "I'll take care of the door."

Flashing him an appreciative smile, Desiree picked up the receiver.

"We've got another one." Adrian's dark tones shattered the last of her blissful feeling.

While Desiree sank down onto the edge of the bed, Roman looked through the peephole in her door and swore as he viewed the man standing on the front porch. Having no other choice, he opened the door.

"Roman Falconer?"

"You know my name, Detective." A calm born of the knowledge that this moment had been inevitable from the beginning settled over him.

O'Malley's stony expression revealed that he was not in the mood to play games. "I'd like to ask you a few questions, Mr. Falconer," he said, his deep voice ringing out in the small foyer like a death knell. "About the rape and murder of Tabitha Sue Jackson."

A sound, somewhere between a gasp and a whimper, came from behind Roman. With a sinking heart, he glanced back over his shoulder and saw Desiree. Standing in the bedroom doorway, clad in an ivory silk robe, she looked every bit as pale and fragile as the victims of the French Quarter rapist.

14

DESIREE COULDN'T BELIEVE this was happening. After Michael's arrival, at both men's prompting, she'd forced herself to continue with her plan to make coffee. But she went through the motions as if on autopilot.

"Yes, I knew Tabitha," Roman was saying as she returned to the cozy living room with the tray of mugs. Forced to maneuver her way around the spreading branches of the oversize Christmas tree, Desiree thought back to the night Roman had shown up with the tree and realized that was the night she'd fallen in love with him.

"As a client?" the detective asked in a mild, nonjudgmental tone.

"Of course not," Desiree interjected, placing the tray on the coffee table with enough force to send liquid spilling over the tops of the mugs. "I can't believe you'd actually ask a question like that."

O'Malley returned her furious look with a warning one of his one. "Desiree—" he began in a tone she'd heard before.

"Don't 'Desiree' me, Michael Patrick O'Malley." Although she did not lose her temper often, she had a feeling this was about to become one of those rare times when it blew sky-high.

"Desiree." Roman's tone was softer. Gentler. But it, too, carried a warning. "It was a fair question." His weary eyes looked directly at O'Malley. "I've never paid for sex in my life, Detective. Nor did I receive any 'favors' of any kind from Tabitha. We did, however, have several discussions regarding her work. For a book I'm doing." Roman paused, debated mentioning the topic of the book, then decided O'Malley would probably figure it out anyway. "A sequel to the one that's out now."

"*Killing Her Softly.*" O'Malley nodded. "I liked that one. Even if you did tend to make some of those investigators in the district attorney's office look like fools."

A brief smile teased at the corners of Roman's lips. "They say to write what you know."

"Yeah, that's what I've heard." Again O'Malley nodded. "I liked your hero."

That figured, Desiree thought, realizing for the first time exactly how much of Michael O'Malley Roman had put into the dogged detective who'd finally arrested the serial rapist and murderer. That being the case, the irony of the situation did not escape her now.

"Thank you," Roman answered simply.

O'Malley's expression hardened from that of a fan back to that of an interrogating cop. "You realize we have a slight problem here, Mr. Falconer."

"The French Quarter rapist is everyone's problem," Roman answered in a cool, emotionless voice, even as he felt the familiar anvil-like pounding beginning behind his eyes again.

"True. But you're the one who seems to have an interest in rape and murder."

At that, Desiree had to literally bite her lip. Only Roman's reassuring glance kept her from arguing in his defense.

"My royalty statements suggest a great many other people share that interest."

"I suppose I can give you that one." The wicker creaked as O'Malley leaned back in the chair and took a drink of coffee. Although his expression was thought-ful, his pose was relaxed. Watching him, Desiree knew that appearances were deceptive. O'Malley had always been at his most dangerous when he seemed to be at ease.

"However, not all those readers have an intimate . . . Strike that," he corrected at Roman's suddenly sharp look. "A *relationship* with the deceased. And not all of them drive the black Porsche that picked the girl up out-side Armstrong Park the night she was killed."

The words, casually spoken, landed in the middle of the room like a bomb. A silence resembling the after-math of a nuclear explosion settled over the room like a dark cloud.

Unable to remain silent any longer, Desiree said, "There are other black Porsches in this town."

"True. But we have a witness that saw the license plate. A plate assigned to your car," he told Roman.

Roman cursed inwardly. "That's not possible."

"Are you saying you were somewhere else that night?"

"What night?"

O'Malley nodded, silently granting his opponent that point.

"I'll have to check my calendar," Roman said when the detective named the night in question. He already knew the answer. He'd been home the night the unfortunate Tabitha Sue Jackson had been picked up and murdered. Home alone. Lost in a damn bottle.

"I'd appreciate you doing that, Mr. Falconer," O'Mal-ley answered with official politeness.

"It's possible that Roman's car was stolen without his knowledge," Desiree suggested. "The garage isn't at-tached to the house. If he'd been distracted or working or asleep. . . ." Her voice drifted off as she exchanged a quick glance with Roman that told him they were both thinking the same thing. *Asleep? Passed out was a helluva lot more likely.*

"Then, after killing the girl, whoever it was returned the car to the garage?" O'Malley didn't even try to conceal his disbelief about that one.

"It's possible," Desiree insisted, receiving only a grunt in response.

More questions followed. Some about the body that had been discovered last night. The body of a prostitute who'd last been seen the night of the Christmas tour. The night Desiree and Roman had first made love.

Some of the questions were routine, some increasingly intimate. Unfortunately, much of the evidence, while circumstantial, seemed to point directly to Roman.

When the interrogation ended nearly an hour later, Desiree ignored Roman's quiet protest and insisted on walking O'Malley out to his car.

"I can't believe you think Roman could do such a thing," she sputtered.

"If I truly believed the guy was guilty, I'd be arresting him right now, just to keep you from becoming his next victim."

"That's ridiculous. Roman would never hurt me. Besides, in case you've forgotten, I spoke to the rapist on the phone. And he didn't sound anything like Roman."

"Voices can be disguised. And if you'd talked to the rapist on the secured line, we could prove that once and for all with a voice print." For the first time, his own irritation with the situation showed. "But for now we can only work the evidence we've got. And as unpalatable as you might find the idea, it all points to your lover."

"Is that what this is all about?" she demanded hotly. "You're jealous?"

"Hell, no." When she continued to glare at him, he shrugged. "Maybe just a little."

She crossed her arms over her chest. "That doesn't make a great deal of sense, considering your relationship with Karyn."

"You're the one who was always telling me I needed to get in touch with my feelings," he barked. "So, my feelings about you and that mystery-horror writer may not make sense, but it's how I feel, dammit. Just because we're not together anymore doesn't mean I don't care about you, Desiree. Or that I don't remember the good times.

"However," he said, "just because I don't like the guy sleeping with you, there's no way I'd consider him a murder suspect without due cause." He whipped a folded piece of paper out of his pocket. "Check this out."

She took the paper, unfolded it and found herself staring at a black-and-white drawing. "What is this?" she asked, even as her blood, heated by her anger, began to quickly cool.

"It's the police sketch of the guy who ordered those flowers sent to you. The same flowers left with all the victims," he reminded her. "We released it to the press this morning."

The drawing was surprisingly detailed. She could, she considered bleakly, have been looking at a photograph of Roman.

"It's him," O'Malley insisted when she didn't say a word. "And believe me, Desiree, if it weren't for the fact that Falconer was so connected uptown, he'd be behind bars right now."

"He didn't do it."

"I wonder if you'd still say that if you weren't involved with the guy."

"I'm not involved." She folded the paper and unconsciously slipped it into the pocket of her robe. At his arched, argumentative brow, she said, "I'm in love with Roman."

O'Malley's curse was brief and ripe. "I was afraid of that." He gave her a long look. "You remember my beeper number?"

"Of course."

"Do me one favor?"

"If I can."

"Try to think with your head. And not your heart. And if you have the slightest suspicion you might be in trouble, call me?"

As she looked up into his concerned face, Desiree felt horribly torn between the man she'd once tried desperately to love and the man she'd fallen in love with in spite of trying desperately not to. "Roman would never hurt me," she repeated insistently.

He ran the back of his broad hand down her cheek. "I hope you're right." He gave her one last look rife with worry and frustration, then got into his sedan.

Desiree remained on the sidewalk, watching him drive away. Then, with a soft sigh, she returned to the house.

Roman was standing by the window. Desiree knew he'd witnessed O'Malley's tender caress. "He worries about me," she said softly, in way of explanation.

"He's not alone." Once again she looked so delicate. So damned vulnerable.

Roman jammed his hands into the back pockets of his jeans to keep from crushing her to him, to keep from ravishing her here on the flowered needlepoint rug, beneath the oversize Christmas tree, until they could forget they weren't alone. Unfortunately, the French

Quarter rapist had been between them from the beginning.

"I'd better leave."

The finality in his flat tone set off internal alarms. "You're not talking about just for now, are you?"

He was not surprised that she understood his intentions. Desiree's intelligence and insight were two of the many reasons he'd fallen in love with her. "No." He dragged his hands through his hair. "This isn't going to work out."

"It won't if we're not willing to try," she agreed with a calm she was a very long way from feeling. Three weeks ago she'd been trying to convince herself that getting involved with this man would be impossible. Now she realized that it was impossible to imagine a life without him.

She crossed the room until they were standing nearly toe to toe. "One question."

He suspected he knew what was on her mind. "I didn't do it. Any of it."

"I know that." The smile in her still worried eyes flickered. "What I'm a little less sure about is whether you meant what you said earlier." She drew in a nervous breath. "About loving me."

Roman knew he should lie. That he should tell her he'd merely gotten caught up in the moment, after a night of great sex. But looking down into her lovely, open face, a dozen conflicting emotions hit him at once.

"I've never spoken truer words in my life."

Despite the seriousness of their situation, a warm, golden glow spread through her. "Well, then . . ." She pressed her hand against his chest, pleased when his heart began to beat hard and fast beneath her fingertips. "Since you love me—" she kissed his rigid jaw "—and I love you—" she nipped the other side of his jaw "—and we both love each other—" she nuzzled the cleft of his chin "—how about we go back to bed and make love? Then," she suggested silkily, as her lips plucked at his, "we can make plans. What would you say to a New Year's Eve wedding?"

Her breasts were pressed enticingly against his chest, making him ache to taste that delectable flesh. "Wedding?" he asked distractedly as he slipped his hand beneath the lapels of her silk robe.

She arched against his tender touch, her soft sigh becoming a faint moan. "I think it's best, don't you? For the children."

Roman didn't think there was anything left that could surprise him. He caught hold of her hair and lightly urged her head back. "Children?" His dark gaze searched her face, taking in those gleaming eyes, the soft flush adorning her cheekbones, the soft siren's smile that he knew would still possess the power to make him weak when he was a hundred. "Are you—"

"Not yet." She wrapped her arms around him, her silver laugh slipping beneath his skin. "But after the day I have planned for you, Roman Falconer, I'll be amazed if I don't end up carrying your child."

His child. The idea was, Roman realized, incredibly appealing.

He scooped her up into his arms. "You know," he said, as he deftly maneuvered his way past the tree, brushing against a few middle branches, "I always fantasized having a brother or sister."

"Me, too." Despite O'Malley's intrusion on this halcyon time, Desiree felt absolutely giddy.

"That being the case, it would probably be unfair for us to stop with one child."

"Good point. What would you say to three?"

"Three's good." Roman would consider himself blessed to have a single child with this woman.

"Of course, four is a nice, even number," she mused as he lay her on the unmade bed.

"Even numbers are always nice, too."

"My aunt Evangeline had eight kids. And her house was always filled with noise and laughter." A faint sadness crept into her tone.

Hearing it, Roman drew her into his arms and began kissing her temples, her cheeks, her eyelids. "If we're shooting for eight, we'd better get started right away."

Desiree loved the way he could banish the dark clouds. She loved him. "I believe," she said, as she began working on the buttons of his shirt, "that's exactly what I suggested in the first place."

They made love with a sweetness that made Desiree cry. After kissing away her tears, he drew her against him and they fell asleep, making up for the hours they'd missed last night.

When they finally woke, the sun had set and the bedroom was bathed in dark shadows. "It's almost Christmas," Desiree murmured against Roman's chest. "Do you want to exchange presents tonight? Or tomorrow morning?"

They were due at his parents' home for Christmas brunch. The warm family feelings she'd witnessed in the Falconer home, along with the emotions evoked by her very enjoyable lunch with Roman's mother, where she'd learned so much about her mother's early years, had made Desiree resolve to try again with her father's family.

"I've already had all the gifts I could ever want." He pressed his hand against her stomach, imagined his child growing beneath his palm and felt a warm surge of emotion.

"Oh, dear," she complained prettily, "whatever shall I do with the tie and socks I bought you?" She had actually unearthed a leather-bound first edition of Poe's short stories she thought he might enjoy.

"The socks we can take back. As for the tie, I'm sure we can find a use for it." He glanced up at the lacy wrought-iron headboard. "Perhaps I'll use it to keep you in this bed, so you'll be here, right where I want you, whenever I want you."

He spoke without thinking and in jest. But as soon as he heard the words leave his mouth, Roman groaned inwardly. *Smooth move, Falconer.*

"It's not the same," she insisted softly. "What you were talking about and what he does."

She was so sweet. So trusting. Even as he realized how fortunate he was to have found her, Roman knew that it was time—past time—to tell her at least part of the truth.

"I have a confession."

She waited, her eyes unrelentingly calm.

He drew in a deep breath. "I've read your books. *Private Passions* and *Fears and Fantasies.*"

"I know."

Once again she'd managed to surprise him. "For how long?"

"Since that first day. I saw them on your bookshelves and wondered if you knew I'd written them."

"I first saw them on Larry's desk."

"Ah." She nodded. "I should have thought of that possibility. Although I didn't know Larry Kassebaum was your agent."

"One of the things I like about the guy is that he keeps his client list to himself. He didn't tell me about you,"

Roman assured her. "I was just wandering around the office—"

"Snooping, like I was doing in your library," Desiree said with a quick, teasing grin.

"Snooping," Roman admitted with an answering laugh. "I ran across one book and a letter to you in his Out basket. I bought both volumes as soon as I got back to town."

Heaven help her, she had to ask. "And? What did you think?"

"I thought that not only were they well written, the stories spoke to the heart of a fantasy not many people are brave enough to admit to."

"I was amazed at the size of the audience," she responded. "So was Larry."

"I wasn't." Roman ran his hand down her side from her shoulder to her thigh, pleased when he felt the flesh warming beneath his touch. "Did I mention that they were incredibly arousing?"

"No." His touch was proving pretty arousing itself.

"They were. In fact, there was this one particular story, 'Scarlet Ribbons'"

He felt her go momentarily rigid. "Desiree?"

She looked up at him and knew without a shadow of a doubt that she was absolutely safe with this man. "That happens to be one of my personal favorites," she said, putting away any thought of the other man who'd found himself drawn to the erotic story.

Her body, beneath his stroking palm, turned warm and fluid again. She caught his hand and lifted it to her lips. "There is nothing you could ever do that I would say no to, Roman. Nothing."

That declaration, spoken with such sensual conviction, fired Roman's imagination as it burned away the last of his concerns. He bent his head and gave her a dreamy kiss that went on and on, moving his head to change angles, tasting her completely, nibbling, nuzzling, drawing it out with a tormenting tenderness that made her ache.

"Roman..." When he broke off the kiss and stood up, she reached for him, her movements slowed as if in a dream. "Please." She heard her trembling tone, knew she was begging and didn't care. "I want you to make love with me."

"Not yet." He ran the back of his hand down her cheek, her throat. When his thumb lingered at her pulse, she knew he could feel the wild, out-of-control beat of her heart. "There's no hurry."

"That's easy for you to say," she managed to gasp as his hand brushed against her breast and created a flare of heat.

"Easier to say than do," he agreed huskily.

Desiree watched as he crossed her room and plucked a pair of silk scarves—one crimson silk, the other a diaphanous gold-studded chiffon—from the brass hooks. Anticipation flicked through her veins as she realized what he had in mind.

"There's something you have to understand." He was standing beside the bed again, his gaze managing somehow to be both predatory and gentle at the same time. "I'd never—ever—hurt you."

"I know." As she looked up at him, standing over her, strong and hard and unabashedly aroused, she knew that she loved this man irrevocably. And trusted him implicitly.

Roman read the truth in those lovely gold eyes and felt dual waves of relief and desire. "Lord, you are incredible." He took hold of her hand, turned her wrist and pressed his lips against the pale blue vein. "Incredibly beautiful."

Twining the scarlet silk scarf around her wrist, he looped it to the white iron headboard. "Incredibly intelligent." He repeated his actions with the other wrist. "Incredibly sensual."

His gaze swept over her slowly, intimately, the uncensored hunger gleaming in his midnight eyes heating her naked flesh, making her blood pulse. At the same time, she couldn't take her eyes off him. His body was lean. Hard. Blatantly aroused. In spite of all the passion they'd shared during the past two weeks—or perhaps because of it—just looking at him quite literally took her breath away.

He sat down beside her, took her chin in his long fingers, holding her gaze. "I want this to be a night like no other." The husky timbre of his deep voice made her tremble. When he traced a fiery circle around her lips with a finger, they parted softly, invitingly in response.

"A night free of inhibitions." He moistened the fingertip with his tongue and slowly, deliberately drew a line down her throat and around first one sensitive breast, then the other. "A night I can take you in every way I've imagined and bring you only pleasure. A night you can live out your innermost fantasies without guilt or self-recriminations."

"Oh, yes." When his teeth closed around an electrified nipple, Desiree arched her back off the bed. "Yes, to everything."

His hand clenched in her hair, tilting her head back, giving her another one of those long, breath-stealing looks. "Incredible," he murmured once again.

The sunbursts in her liquid eyes gleamed gilt with passion. Never had Roman been so aroused. Never had he been so aware of his power as a man. A surge of savage lust shot through him, his hunger like a wild animal that had been caged up too long finally breaking free of its restraints.

And then his dark head swooped down and he'd fused his mouth to hers. The kiss was hot and ravenous and laced with an edgy, dangerous, thrilling violence that sent tongues of fire licking up between her thighs. She tried to thrust her hands through the jet silk of his hair, belatedly remembering that they were tied.

Never in her life had she been so helpless. Helpless to resist Roman. Helpless to resist her own rising needs. Never had she been more willing to go wherever this man took her. A savage ecstasy was clawing at her, more acute, more erotically intense than anything she'd ever fantasized.

The kiss grew increasingly carnal as his tongue probed deeply, tangling sensuously with hers, tasting the unraveling of her breath, making her moan. His teeth nipped at the sensitive flesh inside her lower lip and made her tremble—not from fear, Roman knew, but from excitement. Expectation.

Need for Desiree burned in him like wildfire. He'd wanted her like this from the beginning, hot and hungry and pleading for more. He wanted her as he wanted no other woman in his life—obsessively, possessively. Dangerously.

All too aware of the incredible gift of trust she'd given him, Roman forced himself to ignore the painful need knotting and twisting inside him. Drawing out the passion that was burning within him, gritting his teeth to keep from exploding, he taunted her mercilessly with his fought-for control as a crescent moon rose in the black winter sky. Her skin, in that cool white light, gleamed like pearls.

He made love to her endlessly, discovering erogenous places Desiree had never known she possessed. She writhed on the hot and tangled sheets, awash in voluptuous anticipation, burning from the inside out, desperate for him to end this torment. She could scarcely breathe from wanting him so badly. And still he continued to drive her closer and closer to the perilous razor's edge of oblivion, goading her into a near frenzy of need.

Roman growled deep in his throat as his open mouth moved over every graceful curve, every sensual hollow. Her flesh was furnace hot, her limbs fluid. Roman had imagined her like this since that first morning she'd shown up at his door. Totally uninhibited. Totally aroused. Totally his.

"Do you have any idea how wonderful you are?" His tongue cut a wet hot swath across her quivering belly. When it dipped into her navel, she moaned and arched her hips off the mattress in a mute plea for fulfillment. "How responsive?"

"Only with you." Her liquid eyes pleaded; her thighs trembled. She was desperate to feel his heaviness against her. She wanted to touch him as he was touching her, make him as crazy as he was making her.

"You are so warm," he murmured, ignoring her ragged request as if she hadn't spoken. His swirling fingers gathered up the hot honey that was flowing between her legs. "So wet." With his eyes locked on hers, he touched his fingertips to his lips. "So wonderful."

With all the power of a conqueror exploring foreign territory, he touched her everywhere, watching her face as she melted like wax in a hot New Orleans summer. Her eyes turned dark and slumberous; her breath rushed between her lips as he continued to caress her with unapologetic carnality.

"Please," she begged raggedly as his questing mouth sent a flick of passion's whip across her moist, heated flesh. Although his caresses remained achingly slow, his wicked hands seemed to be everywhere at once. "I want you."

"I know." He touched his open mouth to her breast. Her heart was a hammer against his lips, sending savage streamers of flame through him, creating an answering surge in his own blood. "I can taste it." His tongue glided down her torso, over her stomach and beyond.

He wanted to bury himself in her heat; he wanted to claim her, possess her, body, mind and soul. He wanted to burn away any memories of any man who had come before. He wanted to ravish her so thoroughly that she could never conceive of any man coming after.

His teeth bit at the vulnerable soft skin at the inside of her trembling thighs, leaving a mark of passion that branded her as belonging to him. Only to him. Forever.

She gasped as the hot tip of his tongue brushed against that ultrasensitive nub of tingling flesh that had been screaming for his touch. Once. Twice. A third time, creating a single shining point of pleasurable, painful delight.

Just when she didn't think she could take any more, his seeking tongue plunged into her center. She was burning alive, her flesh flame, her blood a volcanic torrent raging through her veins.

She sobbed out his name in a hoarse, ragged voice as the flames engulfed her. Before she could catch her breath, he'd jerked the silk restraints free, allowing her to wrap her arms around him as he surged into her.

The liquid fire of her response engulfed him. Entering Desiree was, Roman thought, as the blood swam in his head, like coming home.

Hidden secrets exploded as he filled her. Claimed her. Drove her up again and again.

And finally, when he took her over that last shuddering peak, he followed.

Lids heavy, her body sated, Desiree lay in the protective circle of Roman's arms and waited for her breathing to return to something resembling normal before she even tried to speak.

"I thought I knew," she murmured, her lips against his slick chest. "I believed I could imagine how it would be."

"But?" He pulled her closer and pressed his lips against her tumbled auburn hair.

She smiled up at him, her eyes bright. "I didn't even come close."

"You've no idea what a relief that is."

She laughed at that as she was supposed to. "There's only one problem." She ran her hand down his torso, enjoying the contrast of her pale skin against his dark chest.

Roman sucked in a harsh breath when her fingers skimmed his stomach. "What's that?"

His penis, nestled amidst the ebony curls, was smooth as teak, warm as velvet as it swelled to her caressing touch.

"You spent a very long time driving me crazy." Breathing in the rich, musky scent of their lovemaking, she touched her ravaged lips to his glistening shaft, invoking a low ragged groan that sent a rush of feminine power surging through her. "It seems only fair that I should get equal time."

"You're right." Roman rolled over onto his back and stretched out his arms in a position of surrender. "Have your way with me, sweetheart. I'm all yours."

The wonderful thing was that he was.

So she did.

All night long.

Epilogue

DESIREE WAS FLOATING on air the following morning. Last night had been the most erotic, incredible night of her life. And although it had begun with her sensual surrender, by the time the sun rose, both she and Roman had surrendered ultimate power to the other. And received incomparable rewards in return.

Although she woke to find the bed beside her empty, Desiree didn't worry. Not when she was feeling so wonderfully, thoroughly loved.

She heard him in the kitchen, smelled the rich aroma of freshly brewed coffee and seriously considered, once again, the benefits of spending the rest of her life this way.

"You look like the cat that swallowed the canary," he said as he entered the bedroom, a cup of steaming café au lait in each hand. His lazy, unabashedly sexual gaze skimmed over her. "A sleek, gorgeous feline."

She laughed and accepted the cup he held out to her. "There have been times when you've made me feel like Maggie the Cat," she confessed. "Dancing around on a hot tin roof. But this morning I'm feeling like a plump, lazy tabby."

"Hardly plump." He sat down on the edge of the bed and ran his free hand across her shoulders and over her breasts.

"Not yet." As irrational as it might sound, she knew with an instinctive maternal knowledge that they'd made a baby during the long, love-filled night. She frowned slightly. "Will it bother you? When I'm a fat pregnant lady?"

"A sexy, ripe pregnant lady," he corrected with a look that warmed her all the way to her most feminine core. "All the more to love." The smile faded from his mouth. His eyes. "I do, you know." He ran his palm down her tangled hair. "So very, very much."

"I know." Her own smile faltered as she read the ominous message swirling in his strangely tortured gaze. "And I love you." She caught his hand and held it tightly in hers. "Which is why I think you should tell me what's wrong."

He sighed and looked at the flower-sprigged wall, as if unable or unwilling to meet her eyes. "It's the same thing that's been wrong from the beginning. The same person."

She shook her head. "He doesn't have anything to do with us." Even as she said the words, Desiree knew she was whistling in a graveyard. As if saying it could make it true.

"We can't run away from it any longer, Desiree." He shook his head and closed his eyes for one brief, painful moment. "Not when there's a very good chance that I'll be arrested today."

"Not on Christmas!"

Despite the severity of their situation, Roman couldn't help smiling. "I doubt a holiday will stand in the way of O'Malley doing his job."

"You're not the man he's looking for."

The absolute certainty in her tone gave Roman hope where only weeks ago there'd been none. "You sound so sure of that."

"I am!" She put her cup on the bedside table and got up on her knees, wrapping her arms around his rigid shoulders. "You're a warm and wonderful and loving man, Roman Falconer. You could never rape a woman."

"You can still say that? After last night?"

"Dammit!" She was off the bed in a flash. "I told you, there's no similarity between fantasy and reality." She was pacing, her hands waving like birds, her body quivering with emotion. "You and I made love, Roman. What that sick, murderous pervert does has everything to do with hate."

Looking at her standing there without a stitch of clothing on, radiating passion, love and righteous indignation, her hands on her slender hips, Roman thought yet again that she was the most spectacular creature he'd ever seen.

"How about my car being at the scene?"

"We've covered that. It was obviously stolen while you were inside the house, probably drunk."

He wondered idly at the fact that she'd never questioned why, exactly, he had seen fit to stay as drunk as possible when they'd first met. He reached into his pocket. "How about this?"

She stared at the police sketch. "Where did you get that?"

"I found it on the floor this morning. It obviously fell out of your robe pocket. I suppose you also have an explanation for why the alleged rapist looks like the face I see every morning in the mirror when I shave?"

"Coincidence." She dragged her hair back from her forehead with trembling hands. "Everyone knows police sketches aren't that accurate."

"This one certainly is."

Unfortunately, she couldn't deny that. "They say everyone has a double."

He shook his head, loving this sensual, loyal woman so much that it literally hurt. "One more question."

"Dammit, Roman, it's Christmas. I don't—"

"One more."

She exhaled a long, frustrated breath and plopped down beside him on the bed. "One more."

"You want to tell me why I know what he does? Before he does it? And sometimes while he's doing it?"

The fatal questions, spoken in that low, flat tone, hit her like a body blow to the gut. And the heart. Fortunately, her head remained unaffected.

"That's impossible."

"It should be. If I'm innocent," he agreed. "But if that's the case, then why the hell do I know things about the crimes that the police aren't even revealing?"

"Such as?" She lifted her chin, refusing to believe such a preposterous claim.

"The scarlet ribbons, for one. Ribbons he uses to tie the girls up."

She felt the color literally drain from her face, turning her skin to ice. "You could have guessed," she insisted, her voice not quite as strong as it had been. "From reading my books."

"That's one possibility. But there's more."

She was afraid there would be.

"I saw Tabitha in Whooping Crane Pond." He paused, his eyes and face more grim than she'd ever seen them.

"Before you got that call from your producer reporting that she'd been found."

"That's impossible."

"Not if I'm the killer."

She was on her feet again, emotion bringing much-needed color rushing back to her cheeks. "I told you, there's no way you will ever convince me of that!"

He thought about telling her the rest—how he'd also envisioned her blood on his hands—and decided he'd dumped enough reality on her for one day.

"As much as I appreciate your unwavering belief in my innocence—"

"It's the truth." She dropped to her knees beside the bed and wrapped her arms around him, holding him desperately close. "There are all sorts of explanations," she said in a rush. "You're a writer. A creative person. Undoubtedly more sensitive to emotional vibrations. Perhaps you're picking up on the killer's thought waves—"

"I don't have a satellite dish in my head, sweetheart." Once again her earnestness had his lips curving in a grim smile.

"This isn't funny, Roman!"

"No." He cupped her cheek with his palm. "On that much we can agree."

"We can also agree you didn't do it." When he hesitated, she said, "Because of the last victim. The one Adrian called about yesterday. The one O'Malley asked about. You couldn't have killed her, Roman. Because you were with me the night she was murdered."

Amazingly, he'd forgotten about the most recent murder. As he pondered why, Roman realize it was because he hadn't experienced any mental images. Because his mind had been too filled with Desiree.

"You're right." Relief flooded through him, as cool and clean as a mountain stream. "I couldn't have done it."

"See? I told you." Her smile, warm as it was, wobbled. And her eyes were filled with moisture. "You scared me to death, Roman Falconer."

"I'm sorry." He coaxed her onto his lap and held her tightly, as if she were his very own talisman. "There's still a very good chance I'll be arrested."

"Not if they catch the killer first."

"They haven't yet," Roman felt obliged to reply.

"True." She chewed thoughtfully on her lower lip. "Roman, I just had an idea—"

"No!" His shout echoed around them in the close confines of the cozy bedroom. "You are not going to do a single thing to try to lure this crazy out of hiding. It's too damn dangerous."

He should have told her about the vision, Roman decided.

"Don't worry." She pressed a quick, reassuring kiss against his lips. "I wasn't thinking any such thing."

Desiree wanted to reassure him, to keep from ruining their first Christmas together.

Roman wanted to be reassured.

But as she kissed him with all the pent-up emotion she was feeling, Desiree knew that there had to be *something* she could do to help this man she loved.

"I REALLY HATE to leave you." Roman's reluctance carved furrows between his dark brows.

They were standing in the front doorway, arms wrapped around each other.

"It's not like you're going to be gone for long." Desiree smiled up at him, rubbing at the deep lines. "After all, how long does it take to pick up a bourbon chocolate pecan pie?" The rich dessert from Brennan's was a staple at the Falconer home on Christmas day. This year Roman had volunteered to pick it up.

"About as long as it takes for you to get into trouble."

She sighed as she viewed the concern in his sober gaze. "For heaven's sake, Roman, now you're sounding exactly like O'Malley."

"That's not so surprising." He skimmed a finger down the slender slope of her nose. "Since we both care a lot about a certain stubborn, risk-taking reporter."

"Will that bother you after we're married? That Michael and I are still friends?"

"Of course not." Roman shrugged. "I've always liked O'Malley. Although I have to admit, I'll like him a helluva lot better when I'm no longer the chief suspect in his murder investigation."

"I'm sure he believes you," Desiree insisted, as if saying it could make true.

"O'Malley doesn't believe anyone. That's what makes him such a good cop."

Church bells chimed, inviting neighbors to Christmas-morning services and reminding Roman and Desiree that time was passing and they were expected at Audubon Park by noon.

"Gotta go." He bent his head and gave her a swift hard kiss that left her head spinning.

Desiree stood in the doorway, watching as he climbed into the damning black Porsche that O'Malley would undoubtedly be impounding before the day was over. She sighed and watched Roman drive away.

She waved to the plainclothes patrolman who was still stationed outside her house and felt a tinge of guilt that he was missing the holiday with his own family.

Then, determined to enjoy this very special day, she went back into the house, smiling as she thought about Roman's reaction when he viewed the drop-dead-gorgeous red velvet dress she'd bought for his parent's Christmas dinner.

She'd finished her shower and was getting ready to blow dry her hair when she heard the familiar sound of the Porsche's engine outside the house. A moment later, she heard the key she'd given Roman turning in the front lock.

"That was certainly fast," she called out. "Did you forget something?"

A frisson of fear raced up her spine when there was no answer. Telling herself that only her imagination was working overtime again, she took a deep breath. "Roman?"

Again there was only silence. She padded quietly across the stenciled floor to the bedside telephone and lifted it gingerly from the receiver.

Nothing.

Another bubble of fear rose in her throat. She forced it down and tried to think.

The house was as still as a tomb. The only sound was the soft cooing of a pigeon outside the bedroom window. The window! Of course, she thought in a rush of relief. She'd just reached it when a familiar voice came from the doorway.

"What are you doing, Desiree, love?"

Her heart in her throat, she turned slowly, biting her lip as she viewed Roman leaning negligently against the door frame.

"You scared me to death!"

"I'm sorry." He smiled—a warm, loving smile designed to coax her into relaxing. "But you're right. I *did* forget something important."

Still uneasy, she watched him carefully, trying to remember that this was the man she loved. The man who loved her. "What's that?"

"This." He took his hand from behind his back. In it he was holding a bloodred rose.

Her blood turned to ice. "You're not Roman."

"Of course I am." His smile was an evil white slash in his dark complexion. "Ask anyone." He began walking toward her. "Ask the florist." Closer. "Or Detective O'Malley." Closer still. "Or how about that cop parked across the street? Who, by the way, said to wish you a very merry Christmas."

Another smile, more wicked than the first. "It seems the man was a fan." He shook his head with mock regret. "He seemed like a very nice man." She watched as he took his free hand out of his pocket, revealing a very lethal switchblade. "It's too bad he had to die. On Christmas."

Horror slashed through her as she viewed the blood on the steel blade.

"What do you want?" She managed, just barely, to force the words past the fear-induced lump lodged in her throat.

"A great many things." He moved closer. "This is, after all, the season for giving." Closer still, allowing her to see the frightening glint of madness in those dark eyes that were mirror images of Roman's. "I suppose we can begin with you."

As he reached for her, Desiree scrambled over the top of the bed in an attempt to escape. But he was quicker, grabbing her arm and throwing her down on the mattress.

"Why are you doing this?"

"Why not?" he asked whimsically with a smile that was a cruel and hateful parody of Roman's loving one. "You're a beautiful woman, Desiree." He trailed the rose down her cheek in a mockery of a caress. "Any man would want you."

It took all her resolve not to tremble at his touch. Desire reminded herself that the key to survival was to remain calm. And to keep him talking until she could figure a way out of this. Or until Roman returned home.

"Most men don't resort to rape." She judged the distance to the door in the event talking wouldn't prove successful.

He laughed at that. "Most men don't know how much you like it rough." He reached into his pocket and pulled out a pair of scarlet satin ribbons. "But *he* does." Pinning her down with a knee to the chest, he took hold of her right wrist and looped one of the red ribbons around it, in much the way Roman had done with her crimson silk scarf. "And I know everything he knows."

Her mouth was dry. Her heart was hammering in her chest. Keep him talking, Desiree reminded herself.

"How?"

"You're a smart lady, *chérie*. Haven't you figured it out yet?" He'd dropped Roman's cultured Southern accent, and in its place she recognized the familiar cadence of the bayou.

She stared up into this face that was a carbon copy of the man she loved and remembered what Roman had told her about being adopted the night she'd cooked pasta for them. "Oh, my God," she breathed. "You're his brother."

"His twin," he agreed with another one of those wicked smiles that slashed at her like the blade of the knife he still held in his hand. "I guess you'd call me his evil twin." This time his laugh was high-pitched, leaving Desiree with not a single doubt that this was a very sick man.

"I don't understand." He'd yet to tie the ribbon to the headboard. Desiree's only hope was that she could distract him long enough to escape. "I know Roman was adopted, but—"

"Not just Roman!" he shouted, leaving the bed to begin pacing furiously, his fist curled around the flower. "We were both adopted out by the *putain* who gave birth to us."

From her years of European boarding schools, Desiree knew more than a little street French. But even so, she wouldn't have needed a translator to know that he'd just called his mother—and, if he could be believed, Roman's mother—a whore.

"I'm sorry," she murmured.

"You're sorry?" He spun around and jammed his fist into the wall directly above the headboard, making her flinch. His face was twisted into the most hideous mask she'd ever seen. At this moment, he looked nothing like Roman. "Who the hell are you to be sorry for me? You're just another bitch who'll spread her legs for any man that comes along."

He swung again, this time a harsh, backhanded blow to her cheek that sent her head reeling and made her see stars.

Tears sprang to her eyes, but Desiree refused to cry. "I'm not your mother," she said, hoping she could reason with him until Roman returned. How long could it take to pick up a pecan pie?

"You're just like her." He'd begun to pace again. "I saw you." When he stopped beside the bed and glared down at her, she knew, all too well, how Tabitha Sue Jackson and all the others had felt when they'd realized what a mistake they'd made in going off with this man. "I saw you with that cop, outside, wearing nothing but this robe."

He ripped it open, exposing her to his blazing, mad gaze. "You'd just finished screwing one lover and you were coming on to another." He threw a handful of crushed, dark crimson rose petals onto her body.

"I really am sorry for whatever has happened to you," she began, once again trying for reason, "but—"

"I don't want your damn pity!" he roared, hitting her again, this time with a powerful fist to her temple that caused a wavy black haze to swim in front of her eyes.

He began to shout a stream of obscenities interspersed with a long, rambling monologue about how, due to a stroke of luck, Roman had ended up with a wealthy family who'd given him everything, while he'd been sold off to a violent, alcoholic sugar cane farmer who'd only wanted another pair of hands to work from dawn to dusk.

It wasn't fair, he ranted. But now he was going to even the score. Once and for all.

"I'm going to have you, *chérie.* The way you like it, hard and violent until you're screaming that pretty red head off. And when I'm done, you're going to realize that I'm better than Roman Falconer could ever be.

"And then, unfortunately, I'm going to have to kill you. So my rich, famous brother will hang for your murder. And the murder of all those other whores."

His voice, loud as it was, sounded as if it was coming from a very long way away. Desiree struggled to remain conscious even as she felt herself succumbing to the darkness. She was just about to go under when, as impossible as she knew it to be, she felt the hours-old life inside her stir.

Dispensing with reason, she began to fight. To save herself, but most of all, to save her unborn child. The child she'd made with Roman.

The rapist was back on the bed, kneeling over her, tying her to the lacy wrought-iron headboard. Shouting at the top of her lungs, Desiree jerked her knee up between his legs, causing him to roar like a wounded lion as he rolled on the mattress, holding his hands over his groin.

She was off the bed in a flash, pulling open the dresser drawer to retrieve the gun O'Malley had given her. The gun she had forgotten about until now. Then she turned and ran from the room.

She was halfway down the hall when he caught up with her. Grabbing her by her streaming hair, he threw her to the floor. She dropped the pistol, but, crawling, managed to retrieve it. Her fingers had just curled around the grip when the toe of his boot slammed into her rib cage.

"Stop it!" she shouted, ignoring the blinding pain as she pointed the gun up at him. Her hands were shaking like a leaf in a Gulf Coast hurricane. "Or I'll shoot!"

His only answer was a blood-chilling laugh. When he swung his foot back to kick her again, Desiree closed her eyes and pulled the trigger. The report was deafening. It also was ineffective, hitting the wall behind him.

Her head was swimming and her chest felt as if it were on fire. But she managed to keep her eyes open this time as she pulled the trigger and another shot ripped the air. Desiree watched the shocked look come across his face and viewed the dark red stain on his thigh.

He screamed a curse. But like the monster from every horror movie she'd ever seen, he kept coming.

She pulled the trigger one more time.

Nothing.

Having no idea what to do with a jammed pistol, she scrambled frantically to her feet and resumed running for the front door. She just barely squeezed by the Christmas tree, then, in one final act of desperation, knocked it over, blocking her attacker's way into the living room.

Vertigo was crashing down on her, causing her knees to give way beneath her. Crawling again, she managed to cross the small room and was just reaching up for the antique brass knob when the door swung open.

"Roman!" Relief was instantaneous.

He gathered her into his arms, pulling her out of the way of O'Malley, who succeeded in stopping Desiree's deadly assailant with one expertly placed shot.

"IT'S ALL RIGHT," Roman was saying over and over again, his lips raining desperate kisses over her bruised face. "You're going to be all right."

Believing him absolutely, trusting him implicitly, Desiree lifted a hand to his cheek and smiled. "I can't believe I'm spending Christmas in the hospital," she complained.

"You have a concussion. The doctor wants to keep you overnight for observation."

"Why can't we just go home? And *you* can watch me."

He ran a hand down the side of her face and tamped down the rage he felt when he viewed the ugly dark bruises. His first emotion, when he'd he'd come out of the restaurant to find his car stolen, had been irritation.

An instant later, sheer terror had torn through him when he realized the theft was no annoying coincidence. His car had obviously been taken to keep him from returning to Desiree!

Dropping the pie, he'd raced back into the restaurant and called 911, instructing the dispatcher to contact O'Malley and send cops over to Desiree's Irish Channel address. Then, borrowing the restaurant owner's car, he'd sped to the house and was running up the sidewalk to the front door when O'Malley arrived, followed by three squad cars. And a SWAT/hostage team that fortunately did not prove necessary.

"I intend to spend the rest of my life doing exactly that," he assured her. "Beginning with tonight. I'm going to be sitting right beside the bed. All night long."

"I can think of a lot of other things I'd rather be doing all night long with you."

Her saucy grin revealed that she'd come through the ordeal with her indomitable spirit intact. Roman would have expected nothing less.

"That's tomorrow night."

"Something wrong with tomorrow morning?"

He laughed, enjoying the release. "Whatever you want." He sat down on the edge of the too narrow bed and drew her into his arms. "I'm sorry."

She looked at him in surprise. "It certainly wasn't your fault."

"O'Malley still hasn't found out who the guy was. But if he does turn out to be a brother I never knew I had—"

"Which might explain you knowing what he was doing," Desiree pointed out. "I've read about strange mind links between identical twins."

"Believe me, I've already considered that." The extra car keys—which Roman had never noticed were missing from his desk drawer—had been found in the rapist's pocket. Having the keys would have made it a simple matter to not only take the Porsche, but to slip into the house and read the book, as it progressed, on Roman's computer.

What Roman knew no one would ever be able to satisfactorily explain was how he'd known what the monster was thinking.

Wanting nothing more than to put all this behind him, he dragged a weary hand down his face. "As eerie as the idea is, you might be on to something."

"I suppose it'll make a good story."

"For someone else to tell." Roman knew he'd never completely get over the absolute terror he'd felt when he arrived at the house to hear Desiree's scream. And those gunshots. "There's no amount of money that would make me willing to relive today."

"That makes two of us," she said, secretly relieved by his decision. "We were lucky that O'Malley's timing was so good. Showing up when he did."

"Lucky," Roman agreed, thinking that if O'Malley hadn't killed the monster, he would have happily done the deed himself with his bare hands.

He cupped the unbruised side of her face in his palm and gave her a long kiss wrought with relief and passion and most of all, love.

"You'd better eat your dinner," he said, nodding at the tray on the rolling table. "Before it gets cold."

"At least I don't have to have the typical hospital turkey roll." Desiree took a bite of the roast goose Roman's mother had sent over to the hospital. "Although I'm really sorry I'm missing your mother's dinner party."

"So was she. But fortunately, her guests have agreed to stay a few more days. We figured it didn't make much sense for them to drive all the way home to Iberville, then come back in a few days for our wedding."

"Iberville?" Her eyes widened as his words sank in. "Are you saying that your mother's Christmas dinner guests are—"

"The entire Dupree clan. Who are, by the way, all waiting outside to see you."

"Oh, Roman." It was, Desiree decided, the most perfect gift anyone could ever have given her.

As Roman drew her into his arms for a deliriously sweet kiss, her eyes filled with tears of wonder. Tears of joy.

Outside the hospital room, holiday lights glittered gaily along St. Charles Avenue, twinkled amidst the towering oaks of City Park, sparkled from the famed wrought-iron railings, flashed on the sides of the historic streetcars, blazed from the *Creole Queen* on the river. Christmas carols melded with the melancholy blues and jazz, delighting citizens and visitors alike with promises of sleigh bells, herald angels and miracles.

Inside the hospital room, Roman and Desiree made their own sweet music as they celebrated the very special miracle of love.

HARLEQUIN®

Temptation

Secret Fantasies

Do you have a secret fantasy?

Holly Morris does. All she'd ever wanted was to live happily ever after with the man she loved. But a tragic accident shattered that dream. Or had it? Craig Ford strongly reminds her of her former lover. He has the same expressions, the same gestures…and the same memories. Is he her fantasy come to life? Find out in #566, LOOK INTO MY EYES by Glenda Sanders, available in December 1995.

Everybody has a secret fantasy. And you'll find them all in Temptation's exciting yearlong miniseries, **Secret Fantasies.** Throughout 1995, one book each month focuses on the hero and heroine's innermost romantic desires.…

SF-12

Take 4 bestselling love stories FREE

Plus get a FREE surprise gift!

Special Limited-time Offer

Mail to Harlequin Reader Service®

3010 Walden Avenue
P.O. Box 1867
Buffalo, N.Y. 14269-1867

YES! Please send me 4 free Harlequin Temptation® novels and my free surprise gift. Then send me 4 brand-new novels every month, which I will receive before they appear in bookstores. Bill me at the low price of $2.66 each plus 25¢ delivery and applicable sales tax, if any.* That's the complete price and a savings of over 10% off the cover prices—quite a bargain! I understand that accepting the books and gift places me under no obligation ever to buy any books. I can always return a shipment and cancel at any time. Even if I never buy another book from Harlequin, the 4 free books and the surprise gift are mine to keep forever.

142 BPA AW6V

Name	(PLEASE PRINT)	
Address	Apt. No.	
City	State	Zip

This offer is limited to one order per household and not valid to present Harlequin Temptation® subscribers. *Terms and prices are subject to change without notice. Sales tax applicable in N.Y.

UTEMP-995   ©1990 Harlequin Enterprises Limited

MOVE OVER, MELROSE PLACE

Come live and love in L.A. with the tenants of Bachelor Arms. Enjoy a year's worth of wonderful love stories and meet colorful neighbors you'll bump into again and again.

From Judith Arnold, bestselling author of over thirty-five novels, comes the conclusion to the legend of Bachelor Arms. Whenever a resident sees "the lady in the mirror," his or her life is changed and no one's more so than Clint McCreary's. Or Hope Henley, who looks exactly like the mysterious woman. Don't miss Judith Arnold's captivating:

#561 THE LADY IN THE MIRROR (November 1995)

#565 TIMELESS LOVE (December 1995)

Believe the legend...

URBAN
COWBOYS

A Stetson and spurs don't make a man a cowboy.

Being a real cowboy means being able to tough it out on the ranch and on the range. Three Manhattan city slickers with something to prove meet that challenge...and succeed.

But are they man enough to handle the three wild western women who lasso their hearts?

Bestselling author Vicki Lewis Thompson will take you on the most exciting trail ride of your life with her fabulous new trilogy— Urban Cowboys.

THE TRAILBLAZER #555 (September 1995)

THE DRIFTER #559 (October 1995)

THE LAWMAN #563 (November 1995)

HARLEQUIN®

Temptation®

You're About to Become a *Privileged Woman*

Reap the rewards of fabulous free gifts and benefits with proofs-of-purchase from Harlequin and Silhouette books

Pages & Privileges™

It's our way of thanking you for buying our books at your favorite retail stores.

PROOF OF PURCHASE
HT-PP73
Offer expires October 31, 1996

Pages & Privileges™

**Harlequin and Silhouette—
the most privileged readers in the world!**

For more information about Harlequin and Silhouette's PAGES & PRIVILEGES program call the Pages & Privileges Benefits Desk: 1-503-794-2499

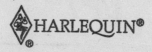

HARLEQUIN®

HT-PP73